George Peele's Edward I: A Retelling

David Bruce

Published by David Bruce, 2022.

GEORGE PEELE'S EDWARD I: A RETELLING

First edition. July 20, 2022.

Copyright © 2022 David Bruce.

ISBN: 979-8201290641

Written by David Bruce.

Table of Contents

Dedication

Dedicated to Carl Eugene Bruce and Josephine Saturday Bruce

My father, Carl Eugene Bruce, died on 24 October 2013. He used to work for Ohio Power, and at one time, his job was to shut off the electricity of people who had not paid their bills. He sometimes would find a home with an impoverished mother and some children. Instead of shutting off their electricity, he would tell the mother that she needed to pay her bill or soon her electricity would be shut off. He would write on a form that no one was home when he stopped by because if no one was home he did not have to shut off their electricity.

The best good deed that anyone ever did for my father occurred after a storm that knocked down many power lines. He and other linemen worked long hours and got wet and cold. Their feet were freezing because water got into their boots and soaked their socks. Fortunately, a kind woman gave my father and the other linemen dry socks to wear.

My mother, Josephine Saturday Bruce, died on 14 June 2003. She used to work at a store that sold clothing. One day, an impoverished mother with a baby clothed in rags walked into the store and started shoplifting in an interesting way: The mother took the rags off her baby and dressed the infant in new clothing. My mother knew that this mother could not afford to buy the clothing, but she helped the mother dress her baby and then she watched as the mother walked out of the store without paying.

My mother and my father both died at 7:40 p.m.

Cover Illustration for George Peele's *Edward I*: A Retelling:
Public Domain
https://commons.wikimedia.org

***

Educate Yourself
    Read Like A Wolf Eats
    Be Excellent to Each Other
    Books Then, Books Now, Books Forever

***

In this retelling, as in all my retellings, I have tried to make the work of literature accessible to modern readers who may lack some of the knowledge about mythology, religion, and history that the literary work's contemporary audience had.

Do you know a language other than English? If you do, I give you permission to translate this book, copyright your translation, publish or self-publish it, and keep all the royalties for yourself. (Do give me credit, of course, for the original retelling.)

I would like to see my retellings of classic literature used in schools, so I give permission to the country of Finland (and all other countries) to give copies of this book to all students forever. I also give permission to the state of Texas (and all other states) to give copies of this book to all students forever. I also give permission to all teachers to give copies of this book to all students forever.

Teachers need not actually teach my retellings. Teachers are welcome to give students copies of my books as background material. For example, if they are teaching Homer's *Iliad* and *Odyssey*, teachers are welcome to give students copies of my *Virgil's* Aeneid: *A Retelling in Prose* and tell students, "Here's another ancient epic you may want to read in your spare time."

CAST OF CHARACTERS

The English Royal Family:

Edward I, King of England, nicknamed "Longshanks" because of his height. He was six-foot-two, which was impressive in the 1200s. His wife often calls him "Ned." His father was King Henry III.

Queen Eleanor, Edward's consort. She is Eleanor of Castile. Her husband often calls her "Nell."

Katherine, Eleanor's Attendant. Queen Eleanor, who is from the Kingdom of Castile, calls her Katherina.

Joan of Acre, their daughter. She was born in Acre, a city in Israel.

Edward, Prince of Wales, son of King Edward I and Queen Eleanor. He is born during the course of the play, and he later becomes King Edward II.

Queen-Mother, consort of the deceased Henry III. She is Eleanor of Provence.

Edmund, Duke of Lancaster, Edward's brother. "Mun" was King Edward I's nickname for Edmund.

Duchess of Lancaster, Edmund's wife.

English Nobility:

Gilbert de Clare, Earl of Gloucester.

Earl of Sussex.

Sir Roger Mortimer, Earl of March.

Sir Thomas Spencer.

Cressingham, a noble.

Other English Characters:

Bishop.

Mayoress of London. Her name is Mary.

Lady Eleanor, daughter of Simon de Montfort, the Duke of Leicester. Marries Llewelyn, Prince of Wales.

Potter's Wife.

John, Servant to Potter's wife.

The Welsh:

Llewelyn, Prince of Wales.

Sir David of Brecknock, Llewelyn's brother.

Rice ap Meredith, a Baron.
Owen ap Rice, a Baron.
Friar Hugh ap David.
Guenthian, the Friar's wench.
Jack, Novice of the Friar.
Guenther, a Messenger.
Morgan Pigot the harper. Engages in prophecy.
Farmer.

The Scots:

John Baliol, elected King of Scotland.
Versses, a Lord.
Lord Bruce, one of Baliol's attendants.

Others:

English Lords, Scottish Lords, Welsh Barons, Ladies, Messengers, Soldiers, etc.

NOTES:

King Edward I's life dates are June 1239 – 7 July 1307. He became King when his father died on 16 November 1272, and he was crowned on 19 August 1274 after returning from the Ninth Crusade.

Peter Lukacs has an excellent annotated text of the play at ElizabethanDrama.org. It can be downloaded free:

http://elizabethandrama.org/wp-content/uploads/2019/10/Edward-I-Annotated-B.pdf

https://tinyurl.com/y39fp5fg

Also available there is a free theater script of the play.

Nota Bene:

Classicist Alison Parker translated Peele's original Latin clauses. Some of those translations are used in this book.

George Peele assassinates the character of Queen Eleanor, Edward's consort. She was Eleanor of Castile, the daughter of the King of Spain, and when George Peele wrote his play in the late 16th century, the English greatly disliked Spaniards.

Another name for Wales is Cambria.

Another name for Britain is Albion.

In Elizabethan culture, a man of higher rank would use words such as "thee," "thy," "thine," and "thou" to refer to a servant. However, two close friends or a husband and wife could properly use "thee," "thy," "thine," and "thou" to refer to each other. A person of lower rank would call a person of higher rank "you."

"Sirrah" was a term of address used when a person of high social status spoke to a male of lower social status.

CHAPTER 1

— SCENE 1 —

At the Royal Palace at Westminster, Gilbert de Clare (the Earl of Gloucester), the Earl of Sussex, Roger Mortimer (the Earl of March), and Sir David (Llewelyn's brother) waited on Eleanor the Queen-Mother.

The Queen Mother, Eleanor of Castile, is the consort of King Henry III and the mother of Edward, who will soon be crowned King Edward I of England.

Gilbert de Clare, the Earl of Gloucester, is a very rich and very powerful 31-year-old man. He has been Regent of England since the death of King Henry III and as such is addressed as Lord Lieutenant.

Roger Mortimer, the Earl of March, is a cousin of Llewelyn, the Welsh rebel, but he is loyal to England.

Sir David is Llewelyn's brother, but he is pretending to support England, although he actually supports Welsh independence.

The time is August of 1274, and Edward, the oldest son of King Henry III, is returning to England after four years of leading a Crusade to the Holy Land and traveling. King Henry III has died, and Edward is now the King of England.

The Queen-Mother said, "My Lord Lieutenant of Gloucester, and Lord Mortimer, to do you honor in your sovereign's eyes, who, as we hear, has newly come on land in England after traveling from Palestine, with all his men-of-war — the poor remainder of the royal fleet, preserved by a miracle in Sicily — go mount your coursers and meet him as he travels on his way here."

Edward had left for the Ninth Crusade in 1270. His fleet of 13 English ships survived a storm at Sicily in 1270, but that storm destroyed many French ships.

Coursers are powerful horses.

The Queen-Mother continued, "Tell him to spur his steed and hurry here. Minutes seem like hours until his mother sees her princely son shining in the glory of his safe return."

Gloucester and Mortimer exited.

The Queen-Mother then addressed the country of England:

"Illustrious England, ancient seat of Kings whose chivalry has royalized and increased your fame — your fame that sounding bravely throughout the world and proclaiming conquests, spoils, and victories rings glorious echoes through the farthest world.

"What warlike nation, trained in feats of arms, what barbarous and uncivilized people, fierce, and untamed, what land under the constellations of the southern part of the world, and what land in the frozen zone under the Sun's wintry glare, recently have not quaked and trembled at the name of Britain and her mighty conquerors?

"Her neighboring realms — Scotland, Denmark, and France — awed with the deeds of Britain's mighty conquerors, and jealous of her arms, have begged defensive and offensive alliances.

"Thus Europe, rich and mighty in her Kings, has feared brave, splendid England and dreaded her Kings.

"And now, to immortalize Albion's champions and make their reputation equal with the Trojans' ancient fame, comes lovely Edward from Jerusalem, veering before the wind and plowing the sea with his stretched sails filled with the breath of men who throughout the world admire his manliness."

Albion is a name for Britain.

The Queen-Mother continued, "And, look, at last arrived at the port of Dover, Edward Longshanks, your King, your glory, and our son, with troops of conquering lords and warlike knights, like bloody-helmeted Mars, surveys his army. He is taller than all the soldiers in his army by the head, and he marches along as bright as the Sun-god Phoebus Apollo's eyes! And we, his mother, shall behold our son, and England's peers shall see their sovereign."

The trumpets sounded, and Edward's soldiers entered the scene.

Edward's maimed soldiers wore helmets and garlands, and every man wore a red cross on his coat.

The ancient — the standard-bearer or ensign — was carried in a chair. He wore a garland and plumes were on his helmet, and he carried the army's banner in his hand.

Gloucester and Mortimer, who were bare-headed, and others followed them.

Arriving last were Edward and his wife Eleanor, Edmund Duke of Lancaster (Edward's brother), and Joan (Edward and Eleanor's daughter), and

Lady Eleanor de Montfort (the daughter of Simon de Montfort, the Duke of Leicester; she was a prisoner who had been captured while trying to sail to Wales), and Almeric de Montfort her brother, with many sailors and soldiers.

The Queen-Mother greeted them: "Gloucester! Edward! Oh, my sweet sons!"

Her sons were Edward and Edmund Duke of Lancaster. Both of them were returning from the Crusade.

Overcome with emotion, she fainted.

King Edward I said, "Help, ladies!

"Oh, ungrateful destiny, which welcomes Edward with this tragedy!"

Gloucester said, "Be patient, your highness. It is only the result of your mother's love overwhelmed with the sight of her thrice-valiant sons."

He then said to the Queen-Mother, "Madam, don't be overwhelmed at seeing his majesty returning with glory from the Holy Land."

The Queen-Mother said, "Brave sons, the worthy champions of our God, the honorable soldiers of the Highest, bear with your mother, whose abundant love with tears of joy salutes your sweet return from famous journeys that were both hard and fortunate.

"But, lords, alas, how heavy is our loss since your departure to these Christian wars! The King your father, and the Prince your son, and your brave uncle, Almain's Emperor, woe to me, are dead!"

Henry III, Edward's father, died on 16 November 1272.

Edward and Eleanor's first son, John, who was born in 1266, died on 3 August 1271.

King Edward I's uncle, Richard of Cornwall, who had served as Emperor of the Holy Roman Empire, died on 2 April 1272.

Almain is a name for Germany.

"Take comfort, madam," King Edward I said. "Leave these sad laments. Dear was my uncle, dearer was my son, and ten times dearer was my noble father. Yet, even if their lives were valued at a thousand worlds, they cannot escape the arrest of dreadful Death, Death who seizes and summons all alike.

"So then, leaving them to heavenly blessedness, to join in thrones of glory with the just, I salute your royal majesty, my gracious mother-Queen, and you, my lords, Gilbert de Clare, Sussex, and Mortimer, and all the princely states of England's peers, with health and honor to your hearts' content.

"And welcome are you, wished-for England, on whose ground these feet so often have desired to tread."

He then addressed his wife, Queen Eleanor, who had traveled with him to the Holy Land for the Crusade and whose nickname was Nell: "Welcome, sweet Queen, my fellow-traveler. Welcome, sweet Nell, my fellow-mate in arms, whose eyes have seen the slaughtered Saracens piled in the ditches of Jerusalem."

Saracens were those who opposed the Crusaders in the Holy Land.

King Edward I continued, "And lastly welcome, manly followers, who bear the scars of honor and of arms, and on your war-drums carry crowns as Kings — crown mural, naval, and triumphant all."

A crown mural was a gold crown that was awarded to the first man to scale a wall of a besieged town. It was decorated with battlements.

A naval crown was a gold crown that was awarded to the victor of a naval battle. It was decorated with the beaks of ships.

A triumphant crown was a triumphal crown that was awarded to victorious generals.

King Edward I continued, "At the sight of you, the trembling Turks have fled like sheep before the wolves, and Saracens have made their cottages in walled towns. But bulwarks had no force to beat you back.

"Lords, these are soldiers who will enter brass gates and tear down lime and mortar with their fingernails. Embrace them, barons. These soldiers have gotten the name of English gentlemen and knights-at-arms. Not one of these but in the open battlefield has won his crown, his ornamental chain of knighthood, and his spurs. Not Caesar, leading through the streets of Rome in triumph the captive Kings of conquered nations, was in his princely triumphs honored more than English Edward in this martial sight."

Many of his soldiers had lost arms or legs in battle. Edward I now addressed them: "Countrymen, your limbs were lost in service of the Lord, Who is your glory and your country's fame. In replacement of your limbs, you shall have pensions, lordships, and lands, and you will be my counsellors in the affairs of war.

"Soldiers, sit down.

"Nell, sit by my side.

"These soldiers are Prince Edward's splendid treasury."

The Queen-Mother sat on one side, and Queen Eleanor sat on the other. King Edward I sat in the middle. He was mounted highest, and at his feet the standard-bearer sat.

King Edward I said, "Oh, glorious Capitol! Beauteous Senate-house! Triumphant Edward, how, like sturdy oaks, do these your soldiers circle around you to shield and shelter you from winter's storms!"

He now singled out two soldiers: old Aimes of the Vies and Matrevers.

"Display your cross, old Aimes of the Vies.

"Beat on your drums, tanned with India's Sun, my lusty western lads.

"Matrevers, you sound on your trumpet proudly here a perfect piece of military music in honor of your sovereign's safe return.

"Thus Longshanks bids his soldiers, *Bien venu*."

"*Bien venu*" is French for "welcome."

Soldiers played drums and trumpets and waved flags.

King Edward I continued, "Oh, God, my God, the brightness of my day, how often have You preserved Your servant and kept him safe, by sea and by land, yea, in the gates of death! Oh, God, to You how highly am I bound for setting me with all these others on English ground!

"One of my mansion-houses will I give to be a hospital for my maimed men, where everyone shall have a hundred marks of yearly pension for his maintenance."

"Marks" are units of money.

King Edward I continued, "A soldier who fights for Christ and country shall lack no pension while King Edward lives.

"Lords, you who love me, now be liberal and generous and give your gift to these maimed men."

He was asking for contributions of money from the lords of England to provide services and pensions to the maimed soldiers.

The Queen-Mother said, "Towards this purpose your mother gives, out of her dowry, five thousand pounds of gold to find them surgeons to heal their wounds. And while this ancient standard-bearer lives, he shall have forty pounds for a yearly pension — and to be my beadsman, father, if you please."

In this society, people called old men, even those to whom they were not related, "father."

The standard-bearer, who was old, nodded his assent.

A beadsman is paid to say prayers for someone.

King Edward I said to his mother, "Madam, I tell you that England never bred a better soldier than your beadsman is — and that is something the Sultan and his army felt in the Crusade."

Edmund Duke of Lancaster said, "Out of the Duchy of rich Lancaster, to find soft bedding for their bruised bones, Duke Edmund gives three thousand pounds."

King Edward I said, "Thank you, brother Edmund. Happy is England under Edward's reign, when men are held so highly in regard that nobles compete over who shall remunerate and reward the soldiers' resolution and courage with their regard.

"My Lord of Gloucester, what is your benevolent gift?"

Gloucester answered, "A thousand marks, if it please your majesty."

"And yours, my Lord of Sussex?" King Edward I asked.

"Five hundred pounds, if it please your majesty," the Earl of Sussex replied.

"What do you say, Sir David of Brecknock?" King Edward I asked.

Sir David replied, "Sir David cannot be too liberal to a soldier, yet so that I may give no more than a poor knight is able, and not presume as a mighty Earl, I give, my lord, four hundred, fourscore, and nineteen pounds."

Sir David was Welsh and "only" a knight, and he did not want to outshine any of the English lords, and so he pledged to give 499 pounds, one pound less than the Earl of Sussex had pledged.

Sir David said, "And so, my Lord of Sussex, I am behind you an ace."

"And yet, Sir David," the Earl of Sussex said, "you amble after me apace."

The word "amble" means "stroll," while the word "apace" means "speedily."

In other words, Sir David was right behind him in giving and in giving quickly.

King Edward I said, "Well said, David; you could not be a Camber-Briton if you did not love a soldier with your heart."

"Cambria" is a name for Wales.

King Edward I then said, "Let me see now if my arithmetic will serve to total the particulars."

His wife, Queen Eleanor, said, "Why, my lord, I hope you mean I shall be a benefactor to my fellow-soldiers."

She also wanted to contribute to the soldiers' welfare.

"And well said, Nell!" King Edward I said. "What do you want me to set down for your pledge?"

Queen Eleanor said, "No, my lord. I am old enough to set my pledge down for myself. You will allow what I do, won't you?"

"That I will, madam," King Edward I said, "even if your pledge were to the value of my kingdom."

"What is the sum that has been pledged, my lord?" Queen Eleanor asked.

King Edward I answered, "Ten thousand pounds, my Nell."

Queen Eleanor said, "Then, Eleanor, think of a gift worthy of the King of England's wife and the King of Spain's daughter, and give such a largess — generous gift — that the chronicles of this land may crow and boast about the record of your generosity.

"*Parturiunt montes, nascetur ridiculus mus.*"

The Latin means, "The mountains are in labor, a ridiculous mouse will be born." In other words, much is promised, but little will be delivered.

She then added a cipher — a zero — at the end of the number of pounds that had been pledged, thereby turning 10,000 into 100,000.

Queen Eleanor said, "There, my lord: neither one, two, nor three, but a poor zero to enrich good fellows, and compound their figure in their kind."

The zero would enrich the soldiers and raise their social status.

King Edward I said, "Madam, I commend your writing and your pledge. It is evidence of your honorable disposition. Sweet Nell, you would not be you with your high-mounting mind if your gift to the soldiers did not surpass all the rest of the gifts."

Gloucester said, "Do you call this a *ridiculus mus*? By the Virgin Mary, sir, this mouse would make a foul hole in a fair cheese. It is only a zero, but it has made of ten thousand pounds a hundred thousand pounds."

A hundred thousand pounds is a lot of money now, and it was a very enormous sum in the Middle Ages. The King would have to raise the money by raising taxes on his people, thus burdening his country.

The King's brother, Edmund Duke of Lancaster, said, "It is a princely gift and a worthy memory."

Gloucester said, "My gracious lord, since earlier I was assigned Lieutenant to his majesty, here I render up the crown, which was left in charge with me by your princely father King Henry, who on his death-bed continually called for you, and dying willed to you the diadem."

Gloucester had been a regent of England since the death of Edward's father: King Henry III.

"Thanks, worthy lord," King Edward I said. "And seeing that it is decreed by the judgment of the heavens, and seeing that it is a lawful line of our succession, unworthy Edward has become your King. We take it as a blessing from on high. And we order that our coronation will be solemnized upon the next fourteenth of December."

"Upon the next fourteenth of December!" Queen Eleanor exclaimed. "Alas, my lord, the time is all too short and sudden for so great a ceremony.

"A year would be scarcely enough to set to work tailors, embroiderers, and men of rare device in fashion for the preparation of clothing of such great estate.

"Trust me, sweet Ned, hardly shall I have time in twenty weeks to decide what fashion of robes to wear. I ask you, please, then, to defer your coronation until the spring, so that we may have our garments perfect in all details.

"I intend to send to Spain for tailors, who together with those who are our most cunning English tailors shall provide some fantastic suits of clothing for us."

Using the King's nickname, Queen Eleanor then said, "Why, let me show off now or never, Ned!"

"Madam, be content," King Edward I said. "I wish that this were my greatest worry! You shall have garments to your heart's desire. I never read but Englishmen excelled for exchange of rare devices every way. Our English tailors are famous for adapting all kinds of foreign fashion."

Queen Eleanor said, "Yet I ask you, please, Ned, my love, my lord, and King, my fellow-soldier, and companion-in-arms, to do so much honor to your Eleanor, by wearing a suit of clothing that she shall give your grace of her own cost and workmanship perhaps."

They had been to the Crusade together, so Queen Eleanor referred to King Edward as her fellow-soldier and companion-in-arms.

The Queen-Mother said, "The suit of clothing will take a long time to make, daughter-in-law, then, I fear: You are too fine-fingered and fastidious to be quick at work."

King Edward I said, "A greater matter than this would cause no disruption between my Queen and me, and I grant her request.

"Let the suit of clothing for me be such, my Nell, as may be fitting for the majesty and greatness of a King.

"And now, my lords and loving friends, follow your general — me — to the court, after his travels, to rest with him. There we all will recount with pleasure war's alarums, showers, and sharpest storms that have passed."

Everyone except Queen Eleanor and Joan, her daughter, exited.

Queen Eleanor said to herself, "Now, Eleanor, you who are now England's lovely Queen, think of the greatness of your status, and think about how to bear yourself with royalty above the other Queens of Christendom, so that with Spain reaping renown by Eleanor, and Eleanor adding renown to Spain, Britain may admire her — my — magnificence."

She then said to her daughter, "I tell you, Joan, the time has come when our highness — I myself — shall sit as Queen under our royal canopy of state, glistening with pendants of the purest gold.

"Just as if our seat were spangled and decorated all with stars, the world shall wonder at our majesty, our majesty that will be as if the goddess Juno — who was the daughter of eternal Ops, and who turned into the likeness of vermilion-red fumes, where from her cloudy womb the Centaurs leapt — were enthroned in her royal seat."

The royal seat is a throne. Queen Eleanor was looking forward to sitting on a throne and being as royal as Juno, wife of Jupiter, King of the gods.

Ops, who was also known as Rhea, was the mother of some of the Olympian gods, including both Jupiter and Juno, who were brother and sister as well as husband and wife.

Queen Eleanor's knowledge of mythology was lacking. Ixion, King of the Lapiths, wanted to have sex with Juno. Jupiter protected his wife by turning the nymph Naphele into a cloud that resembled Juno. Ixion had sex with the cloud, and from their union came the Centaurs, who were half-man and half-horse. Queen Eleanor's story made it sound as if Juno were turned into a vermilion-red cloud and gave birth to the Centaurs.

Joan replied, "Madam, if Joan your daughter may advise you, don't let your honor make your manners change: Don't become too prideful as Queen. The people of this land are men of war, and the women are courteous, mild, and of gentle temperament. They lay their lives at the feet of Kings who govern them with familiar, friendly majesty. But if their sovereigns once begin to swell with pride, disdaining the commoners' love, which is the strength and sureness of the richest commonwealth, then that King would be better off living a private life than ruling with tyranny and discontent."

Queen Eleanor said, "Indeed, we know them to be headstrong Englishmen. But we shall hold them in a Spanish yoke, and make them know and acknowledge their lord and sovereign. Come, daughter, let us go home in order to provide for all the cunning workmen of this isle who shall be set to work creating fashionable expensive clothing in our great chamber and who shall bountifully feed in my hall.

"My King, like Phoebus Apollo, bridegroom-like, shall march with lovely Thetis to her glassy bed, and all the onlookers shall stand amazed to see King Edward and his lovely Queen sit lovely in England's stately throne."

Her words about Phoebus Apollo the Sun-god and Thetis the sea-nymph and the glassy bed that is the sea were a poetic way of referring to the Sun setting over the ocean. Such Sunsets can be magnificent, and she and the King would look magnificent in their costly clothing at the King's coronation ceremony. They would look as magnificent as the Sun setting over the sea.

CHAPTER 2

— SCENE II —

Llewelyn (the Prince of Wales), Rice ap Meredith, and Owen ap Rice met together at Milford-Haven in Wales. They were carrying swords and small shields that were known as bucklers, and they were wearing close-fitting jackets that were known as frieze jerkins.

Llewelyn had been given the title of Prince of Wales in 1267 in the Treaty of Montgomery when Henry III was King of England, but now he was rebelling against King Edward I.

Rice ap Meredith and Owen ap Rice were noble followers of Llewelyn.

Llewelyn said, "Come, Rice ap Meredith, and rouse yourself for your country's good. Follow the man who intends to make you great. Follow Llewelyn, rightful Prince of Wales, who was sprung from the loins of great Cadwallader, who was descended from the loins of Trojan Brute."

Cadwallader was a Prince of northern Wales in the 12th century.

Brute was supposed to be a great-grandson of Aeneas, a Trojan Prince who survived the fall of Troy and went to Italy and became an important ancestor of the Roman people. Brute went to Britain and became its first King.

Llewelyn continued, "And although the traitorous Saxons, Normans, and Danes have pent up the true remains of glorious Troy within the western mountains of this isle, yet we have hope to climb past these stony pales — these mountains on the border between Wales and England."

The Welsh regarded themselves as the real, original Britons, but invaders — Saxons, Normans, and Danes — had pushed them out of most of Britain and into Wales.

Llewelyn continued, "We hope to lead a Welsh invasion that will amaze the Londoners, as the Romans formerly amazed them, causing them to tremble and cry, 'Llewelyn's at the gate!' To accomplish this, I have brought you forth disguised to the Welsh port town of Milford-Haven to await the landing of the Lady Eleanor."

The Lady Eleanor was the daughter of Simon de Montfort, the Duke of Leicester; she was Llewelyn's new wife. Simon de Montfort had led the barons in their opposition to King Henry III in what was known as the Second Barons' War.

Llewelyn and Lady Eleanor had married by proxy. Someone had stood in for Llewelyn in the marriage ceremony — Llewelyn was not present.

Simon de Montfort died in 1265, King Henry III died in 1272, and the current year was 1274.

Llewelyn continued, "Her delay does make me wonder: The wind is fair, and ten days ago we expected them to arrive here.

"Neptune, god of the sea, be favorable to my love, and steer her ship's keel with your three-forked trident, so that from this shore I may behold her sails, and in my arms embrace my dearest dear."

Rice ap Meredith replied, "Brave Prince of Wales, this honorable match cannot but turn to Cambria's common good."

Cambria was another name for Wales.

Rice ap Meredith continued, "Simon de Montfort, her thrice-valiant sire, who was the general in the Second Barons' War, was loved and honored by the Englishmen. When they hear she's your espoused wife, your grace can be assured that we shall have a great supply of soldiers to mightily make our inroads into England."

Owen ap Rice said, "What we resolved must strongly and aggressively be performed, before King Edward I returns from Palestine. While he wins glory at Jerusalem, let us win ground upon the Englishmen."

The Welshmen had not yet heard that King Edward I had returned from the Crusade. They also had not yet heard that King Edward I had captured Lady Eleanor.

Llewelyn said, "Owen ap Rice, it is that which Llewelyn fears. I fear that Edward will come ashore before we can make provisions for the war. But be it as it will, my brother David is within his court as our spy. He bears a face as if he were my greatest enemy although he is actually on our side. He by this craft shall creep into Edward's heart and give us intelligence from time to time of Edward's intentions, drifts, and stratagems.

"Here let us rest upon the salty seashore, and while our eyes long for our hearts' desires, let us, like friends, entertain ourselves on the sands. Our frolicsome minds are omens for good."

Friar Hugh ap David, Guenthian (who was soon to be his wench, and who was wearing flannel), and Jack (his novice) arrived on the scene. They did not see Llewelyn, Rice ap Meredith, and Owen ap Rice.

Friar Hugh ap David said:

"Guenthian, as I am true man,

"So will I do the best I can.

"Guenthian, as I am true priest,

"So will I be at your behest.

"Guenthian, as I am true Friar,

"So will I be at your desire."

The word "true" means "loyal and faithful."

Jack the novice said:

"My master stands too near the fire.

"Trust him not, wench; he will prove a liar."

Friars are supposed to be celibate, but Friar Hugh ap David had no intention of bring celibate. Because of that, he stood near the "fire" — the wench's vagina. He also stood too near the fire of Hell.

In this society, the word "wench" could be used affectionately.

Llewelyn said, "True man, true Friar, true priest, and true knave, these four in one this trull shall have."

The word "trull" can mean "female prostitute." It can also simply mean "girl."

Friar Hugh ap David said, "Wench, here I swear by my shaven crown — my tonsure — that if I give you a gay green gown, I'll take you up as I laid you down, and never bruise nor batter you."

Prostitutes often wore green gowns. In addition, young men often gave young women green gowns especially in the spring by having sex with them on the grass — the grass stains made their gowns green.

Jack the novice said:

"Oh, don't swear, master. Flesh is frail.

"Wench, when the sign is in the tail,

"Mighty is love and will prevail.

"This churchman is only flattering you."

A sign can point, and so can a penis.

Llewelyn said:

"A pretty worm, and a lusty Friar,

"Who was made for the field, not for the choir."

Friar Hugh ap David was not a good Friar; he would have made a much better farmer.

In this society, "loving worm" was an affectionate reference to a woman.

Guenthian said:

"Mas [Master] Friar, as I am a true maid,

"So do I hold myself by you well paid.

"It is a churchman's lay and verity

"To live in love and charity.

"And therefore I ween [expect], as my creed,

"Your words shall accompany your deed.

"Davy, my dear, I yield in all,

"I am your own to go and come at call."

Guenthian had just agreed to be the Friar's wench and obey his commands.

Rice ap Meredith said, "And so far forth begins our brawl."

A brawl can be a fight or a dance.

Friar Hugh ap David said:

"Then, my Guenthian, to begin,

"Since idleness in love is sin ...."

He then said to Jack the novice:

"Boy, to the town I will have you hie [hurry],

"And so return even by and by [soon],

"When you with cakes and muscadine [a wine],

"And other junkets [delicacies] good and fine,

"Have filled your bottle and your bag."

For the Friar, it was a good time to eat, drink, and be merry with Guenthian.

Jack the novice said:

"Now, master, as I am a true wag,

"I will be neither late nor lag,

"But go and come with gossip's cheer [food and drink for a friend],

"Before Gib our cat can lick her ear.

"For long ago I learned in school,

"That lovers' desires and pleasures cool

"Sans [Without] Ceres' wheat and Bacchus' vine:

"Now, master, for the cakes and wine."

Ceres is the goddess of agriculture and so of the wheat with which we make bread.

Bacchus is the god of grape vines and so of wine.

Friar Hugh ap David said, "Wench, to pass away the time in glee, Guenthian, sit down by me, and let our lips and voices join in a merry country song."

Guenthian said, "Friar, I am at your beck and bay, and at your commandment to sing and say — and to engage in other sports."

Jack the novice exited.

Owen ap Rice said, "Aye, by the Virgin Mary, my lord, this is what a man wants to buy with his money. Here's a wholesome Welsh wench, wrapped in her flannel, as warm as wool and as fit as a pudding for a Friar's mouth.

Friar Hugh ap David and Guenthian sang a country song.

Llewelyn now revealed his and his two followers' presence by saying, "*Pax vobis*! *Pax vobis*! Good fellows, may fair things befall you!"

Pax vobis! is Latin for "Peace to you!"

Friar Hugh ap David said, "*Et cum spiritu tuo*!"

"*Et cum spiritu tuo*!" is Latin for "And with your spirit!"

He meant, "And may peace be with your spirit!"

Friar Hugh ap David continued, "Friends, have you anything else to say to me, the Friar?"

He wanted to be alone with his wench.

Owen ap Rice said, "Much good to you, much good to you, my masters, heartily."

Friar Hugh ap David replied, "And much good to you, sir, when you eat. Have you anything else to say to the Friar?"

"Nothing," Llewelyn said, "but I would gladly know, if mutton is your first dish, what shall be your last service?"

"Mutton" was both a food and a slang word meaning "prostitute" or "woman."

"Service" meant both "course of food" and "religious service."

To "service" an animal is to breed it. When a male animal such as a bull services a cow, the bull covers the cow.

Friar Hugh ap David replied, "It may be, sir, I count it healthy to feed but on one dish at a sitting. Sir, do you wish anything else with the Friar?"

"Oh, nothing, sir," Rice ap Meredith said, "but if you had any manners, you might bid us to fall to with you."

Of course, it is inappropriate to speak like this. For one thing, Jack the novice was unlikely to buy enough food to feed the unexpected "guests."

That is assuming that that "fall to" meant "fall to and eat with you."

But the words could also mean to fall to and help you sexually satisfy your wench — which is also an inappropriate thing to say.

Rice ap Meredith was not above teasing — or perhaps tormenting — the Friar.

Friar Hugh ap David replied, "Nay is the answer; if that is the matter, nay is good enough. Is this all you have to say to the Friar?"

Llewelyn said, "All we have to say to you, sir, is this: It may be, sir, we would walk aside with your wench a little."

More teasing — or tormenting.

Friar Hugh ap David replied, "My masters and friends, I am a poor Friar, a man of God's making, and as good a fellow as you are. I have legs, feet, face, and hands, and heart, from top to toe, on my word, right shape, and Christendom — and I love a wench as a wench should be loved; and if you love yourselves, walk on and go on your way, good friends, please, and let the Friar alone with his flesh."

His flesh was his own flesh — and Guenthian's. It was also the meat that Jack the novice would soon bring.

Llewelyn said, "Oh, Friar, your holy mother, the Church, teaches you to abstain from these morsels."

He meant morsels such as Guenthian.

Llewelyn then said to his followers, "Therefore, my masters, it is a deed of charity to remove this stumbling-block, a fair wench, a shrewd temptation to a Friar's conscience."

Guenthian said, "Friend, if you knew the Friar half as well as the bailiff of the town of Brecknock, you would think you might as soon move the mountain Mannock-deny into the sea as move me, Guenthian, from his side."

The bailiff may have had cause to arrest the Friar a number of times.

Llewelyn said, "By the Mass, and by your leave, we'll prove that we are men."

Guenthian said, "You will try to at your peril, if you try his patience."

Friar Hugh ap David said, "Brother, brother, and my good countrymen —"

Pretending that the Friar was English, Llewelyn interrupted, "Countrymen! No!"

Pretending that he was not Welsh, Owen ap Rice said to Llewelyn, "That's more than you know; and yet, my lord, he might ride, having a filly so near."

A filly is a female horse, but Owen ap Rice was punning: The Friar could sexually ride his filly — his wench.

Owen ap Rice put his hands on Guenthian.

This was taking the "joke" too far.

Ready to fight, Friar Hugh ap David said, "Hands off, good countrymen, I say with few words and fair warnings."

Continuing to pretend that the Friar was an Englishman, Llewelyn said, "Countrymen! We are not so, sir; we renounce you, Friar, and reject your country."

Friar Hugh ap David said, "Then, brother, and my good friends, hands off, if you love your ease."

Rice ap Meredith said, "Ease me no easings. We'll ease you of this carriage."

A "carriage" is a burden: Rice ap Meredith was referring to Guenthian.

Friar Hugh ap David said, "Fellow, be gone quickly, or my pike-staff and I will send you away with a vengeance."

A pike-staff was a walking stick with a metal tip at one end.

Llewelyn said, "I am sorry, trust me, to see the Church so unpatient."

"You dogs, by God's wounds!" the Friar said. "Do me an evil turn and mock me, too? Flesh and blood will not bear this.

"Then rise up, Robert, and say to Richard, *Redde rationem villicationis tuae.*"

The Latin means, "Give an account of your stewardship."

Friar Hugh ap David was talking to Owen ap Rice, who still had his hands on Guenthian. "Richard" was a name that the Friar had given to his walking-stick, and "Robert" may be a name like Tom, Dick, or Harry that he now gave to Owen ap Rice, whose real name he did not know.

"Robert" was challenging "Richard" by seizing the wench. Now "Richard" would have to show that he was a good steward by fighting and defeating "Robert," whose stewardship was bad.

"Stewardship" involves use of authority, and Owen ap Rice was misusing his authority. The Prince of Wales and the Welsh nobles should take care of Welsh citizens, not take advantage of them.

The Friar continued, "Sir countryman, kinsman, Englishman, Welshman, you with the wench, return your *habeas corpus*; here's a *certiorari* for your *procedendo*."

These were legal terms.

Habeas corpus means "produce the body" — that is, hand over a person whom you are unlawfully holding in custody. In this case, it meant: Hand over Guenthian.

Certiorari is a legal order to provide the record of a legal trial that a person involved alleges was not just.

Procedendo is a legal order to retry or resume a legal proceeding.

Friar Hugh ap David then attacked them with his staff.

The "joke" had really gone too far.

"Stop, Friar!" Owen ap Rice said. "We are your countrymen."

Rice ap Meredith pleaded, "Stop! Stop! *Digon*! We are your countrymen, *Mundue*!"

Digon! is Welsh for "Enough!"

Mundue is Rice ap Meredith's Welsh-accented pronunciation of the French *Mon Dieu*! — "My God!"

Still angry, Friar Hugh ap David said, "My countrymen! No, by the Virgin Mary, sir, you shall not be my countrymen."

He said to Llewelyn, "You shall not be my countryman, sir, you, especially you, sir, who spurn the Friar and renounce his country."

Llewelyn said, "Friar, hold your hands and stop attacking us. I swear, as I am a gentleman, that I am a Welshman of high rank, and so are these other two men."

"Of high rank, do you say?" Friar Hugh ap David said. "They who will deny their country are neither gentlemen nor Welshmen.

"Come here, wench. I'll have a bout of fighting with them once more for denying their country."

He assumed an attack position.

Rice ap Meredith said, "Friar, you don't know what you are saying. This is the Prince of Wales, and we are all his attendants, disposed to be pleasant and joke with you a little; but I perceive, Friar, your nose will abide no jest."

Friar Hugh ap David replied, "Jest as much as you will with me, sir, but do not jest on any account with my wench. I and Richard my man here, are here *contra omnes gentes* — that is, against all people."

Friar Hugh ap David and Richard were against all people who would try to take his wench away.

Friar Hugh ap added, "But is this man really Llewelyn, the great Camber-Briton?"

Llewelyn said, "It is he, Friar. Give me your hand, and I thank you twenty times. I promise you that you have cudgeled — beaten — two as good lessons into my jacket as ever any churchman did at so short warning.

"The first lesson is not to be too busy with another man's cattle; the other is not in haste to deny my country."

"To be busy with" was slang for "to have sex with." It also meant "to interfere with."

"Cattle" is similar to "chattel," aka possession. Guenthian was the Friar's wench.

Friar Hugh ap David said, "It is a pity, my lord, but you should have more of this learning — you profit so well by it."

Llewelyn replied, "It is a pity, Friar, but you should be Llewelyn's chaplain because you teach me so well; and so you shall be, by my honor. Here and now I employ you, your boy-servant, and your trull, to follow my fortune *in secula seculorum*."

In secula seculorum is Latin for "for all ages."

Friar Hugh ap David said, "And you hire Richard, my man, sir, if you love me — he who stands by me and has not shrunk at all weathers; and then you have me in my true colors — as I really am."

"Richard" was the name the Friar had given his walking-staff. It had helped and protected him in all weathers — in good times and in bad times and in fights.

Llewelyn said, "Friar, agreed."

Seeing two people coming toward them, Llewelyn ordered, "Rice ap Meredith, welcome the ruffians."

Jack the novice returned, bring with him a harper who sang these words to the tune of "Who List [Enlist or Wish] to Lead a Soldier's Life":

"Go to, go to [Go on, go on], you Britons all,

"And play the men, both great and small:

"A wondrous matter hath befall [has befallen],

"That makes the prophet cry and call,

"Tum date dite dote dum,

"That you must march, both all and some,

"Against your foes with trump [trumpet] and drum:

"I speak to you from God, that you shall overcome."

The harper danced as he sang, turning to the right and then to the left.

The words *Tum date dite dote dum* are simply musical sounds, like Frank Sinatra's *Do be do be do* in "Strangers in the Night."

The harper was also a prophet, apparently prophesizing in his song that Llewelyn would be victorious.

"What now?" Llewelyn said. "Who have we here? 'Tum date dite dote dum'!"

Friar Hugh ap David said, "What! Have we a fellow who dropped out of the heavens? What kind of man is he?"

Rice ap Meredith asked, "Do you know this goosecap?"

A goosecap is a fool.

Friar Hugh ap David said, "What! Not Morgan Pigot, our good Welsh prophet? Oh, he is a holy harper!"

Rice ap Meredith said, "A prophet, with a murrain!"

A murrain is a plague. The words "with a murrain" express astonishment.

Rice ap Meredith continued, "My good lord, let's hear a few of his lines, please."

Jack the novice said, "My lords, he is an odd fellow, I can tell you, as odd as any fellow is in all Wales. He can sing, rhyme with reason, and rhyme without reason, and without reason or rhyme."

"The devil he can!" Llewelyn said. "Rhyme with reason, and rhyme without reason, and reason without rhyme!

"Then, good Morgan Pigot, pluck out your spigot, and draw us a fresh pot from the kinder-kind of your knowledge."

He was using the metaphor of pulling out a spigot from a kilderkin (cask) to allow the ale to flow freely to ask the harper to let his prophecies flow freely.

Friar Hugh ap David said to Llewelyn, "Knowledge it is, my son, knowledge, I assure you."

He then said, "What do you say, Morgan, aren't you a true prophet?"

Morgan Pigot the harper said, "Friar, Friar, I am a prophet truly, for great Llewelyn's love, sent from above to bring him victory."

Llewelyn's love is his new wife: Lady Eleanor.

"Come, then, gentle prophet," Rice ap Meredith said, "and let's see how you can salute your Prince. Say, shall we have good success in our enterprise or not?"

Morgan Pigot the harper prophesied:

"When the weathercock of Carnarvon's steeple shall begat young ones in the belfry, and a herd of goats leave their pasture to be clothed in silver, then shall Brute be born anew, and Wales record their ancient hue.

"Ask Friar David if this is not true."

A weathercock is a weathervane made in the shape of a cock.

"Engender" means "gives birth to."

Brute is a King, and the "Wales record their ancient hue" means the Welsh shall regain their ancient color — independence.

Friar Hugh ap David said to Llewelyn, "This, my lord, he means by you. Oh, he is a prophet, a prophet."

Llewelyn said, "Wait a moment now, good Morgan Pigot, and take us with you a little, please — explain your words. What does your wisdom mean by all this?"

Morgan Pigot the harper said, "The weathercock, my lord, was your father, who by foul weather of war was driven to take sanctuary in Saint Mary's at Carnarvon, where he begat young ones on your mother in the belfry. The young ones he begat were your worship and your brother David."

Llewelyn asked, "But what did you mean by the goats?"

Morgan Pigot the harper replied, "The goats that leave the pasture to be clothed in silver, are the silver goats — the insignia — your men wear on their sleeves."

Friar Hugh ap David said, "Oh, how I love you, Morgan Pigot, our sweet prophet!"

Llewelyn ordered, "Go away, rogue, with your prophecies — get out of my sight!"

Rice ap Meredith said, "Nay, my good lord, let's have a few more of these meters. He has a great supply of them in his head."

Jack the novice said, "Yes, and they are of the best in the market, if your lordship would deign to hear them."

"Villain, go away!" Llewelyn said. "I'll hear no more of your prophecies."

Morgan Pigot the harper prophesied:

"*When legs shall lose their length,*

"*And shanks yield up their strength,*

"*Returning weary home from out the holy land,*

"*A Welshman shall be King*

"*And govern merry England.*"

The prophecy seemed to say that a weary Edward Longshanks would return home to England and Llewelyn would become the King of England.

Rice ap Meredith said to Llewelyn, "Didn't I tell your lordship he would hit it home soon?"

Friar Hugh ap David said, "My lord, he is prophesying about you, that's for certain."

Jack the novice said, "Aye, master — if you mark him, he hit the mark pat."

In other words, "Aye, master — if you pay close attention to him, he hit the center of the target."

Friar Hugh ap David asked, "How, Jack?"

Jack the novice said, "Why, thus:

"*When legs shall lose their length.*

"*And shanks yield up their strength,*

"*Returning weary home from out the holy land,*

"*A Welshman shall be King*

"*And govern merry England.*

"Why, my lord, in this prophecy is your promotion and advancement as plainly seen as a three half-pence through a dish of butter on a Sunny day."

A three half-pence is a coin.

"I think so, Jack," Friar Hugh ap David said, "for he who sees the three half-pence must wait until the butter has melted in the Sun.

"And so, continue, apply yourself, boy. Interpret the prophecy."

Jack the novice said, "*Non ego* — not I, master. You do it, if you dare."

Llewelyn asked Jack the novice, "And so, boy, you mean that he who waits for the fulfilment of this prophecy may see Longshanks shorter by the head and Llewelyn wear the crown in the battlefield?"

"Longshanks shorter by the head" meant that Edward Longshanks would be beheaded.

Friar Hugh ap David said, "By our Lady, the Virgin Mary, my lord, you go near the matter.

"But what more does Morgan Pigot say?"

Morgan Pigot the harper prophesied, "*In the year of our Lord God 1272, shall spring from the loins of Brute, one whose wife's name being the perfect end of his own, shall consummate the peace between England and Wales, and be advanced to ride through Cheapside with a crown on his head.*"

He then interpreted his prophecy: "And that's meant by your lordship, for your wife's name being Ellen, and your own Llewelyn, she bears the perfect end of your own name: so it must necessarily be that, although for a time Ellen flee — that is, is separated — from Llewelyn, you being betrothed in heart each to the other, you must necessarily be advanced to be the highest position of your kin."

"Llewelyn" is pronounced Lou-ellen, and "Eleanor" is pronounced Ellen-or.

If Llewelyn were promoted to the position of the King of England, that would be the highest position ever held by a member of his family.

Llewelyn said, "Jack, I make this prophet your prisoner. Look what way my fortune inclines, for that way goes he."

Jack the novice would be in charge of Morgan Pigot the harper and would do such things as see that he was fed.

Morgan Pigot the harper had prophesied good things for Llewelyn, and if Llewelyn had good fortune, then so would Morgan Pigot. But if Llewelyn had bad fortune, then so would Morgan Pigot. So stated Llewelyn.

Rice ap Meredith said to Friar Hugh ap David, "Sirrah, see you run swiftest."

In other words, go now — quickly.

"Farewell," Friar Hugh ap David said. "I will be far from the spigot."

The spigot was Morgan Pigot the harper, a source of prophecies.

Friar Hugh ap David and Guenthian exited.

Jack the novice said to Morgan Pigot the harper, "Now, sir, if our country ale were as good as your metheglin — your strong Welsh mead — I would teach you to play the knave, or you would teach me to play the harper."

"To play" meant "to act like."

Morgan Pigot the harper said, "*Ambo* — both, boy. You are too light-witted as I am light-minded."

"Light-witted" meant "of low intelligence." "Light-minded" meant "concerned with frivolous things" such as music, perhaps, or "filled with the light of prophecy," or both.

Jack the novice said, "It seems to me that you are very fit and surpassingly well."

Jack the novice and Morgan Pigot the harper exited.

A male messenger named Guenther hastily entered the scene. He was carrying letters.

Llewelyn asked, "What news does Guenther bring with his haste? Say, man, what bodes your message, good or bad? Do you bring good news or bad news?"

Guenther replied, "Bad, my lord. All in vain, I know, you dart your eyes upon the rolling sea, as formerly Aegeus did to behold his son, to welcome and receive your welcome love. And sable — black — sails he saw, and so may you, for whose unfortunate event the salty seas lament."

Aegeus was the father of Theseus, who sailed to Crete to confront the Minotaur, the half-man, half-bull monster that consumed human flesh. Theseus told his father that if he were successful at killing the Minotaur, his ships would sail home with white sails, but if the Minotaur killed him, then the ships would sail home with black sails. He killed the Minotaur but forgot to change the black sails to white sails. His father saw the black sails and committed suicide.

Guenther the messenger then said, "Edward! Oh, Edward!"

Llewelyn asked, "And what about him?"

Guenther said, "He has landed at Dover with his men, returning from Palestine safely. His English lords have welcomed him in triumphant celebrations as if he were an earthly god. He lives to wear his father's diadem and sway the sword of British Albion. He will be crowned King of England."

Albion is another name for Britain.

Guenther the messenger then said, "But Lady Eleanor, your Lady Eleanor!"

Llewelyn said, "And what about her? Has amorous Neptune, god of the sea, gazed upon my love, and stopped her passage with his forked trident? Or, that which I rather fear — oh, deadly fear! — does enamored Nereus withhold my Lady Eleanor?"

Neptune might have stopped Lady Eleanor's ship's passage, or a minor sea-god named Nereus might have fallen in love with Lady Eleanor and taken her to be his consort.

Guenther replied, "Neither Neptune, Nereus, nor any other god withholds from my gracious lord his love. But cruel Edward, that injurious King, withholds your dearest lovely Lady Eleanor.

"Four tall ships of Bristol captured her and Lord Almeric, her unhappy noble brother, as they sailed in a pinnace — a small boat — on the narrow seas of the English channel from Montargis, sixty miles south of Paris, to here. This that I say briefly, these letters tell in detail."

Llewelyn read the letters, which were from his brother Sir David.

Llewelyn said, "Has Longshanks, then, now become so vigorous and active? Has my fair love, my beauteous Lady Eleanor, been captured?

"Villains, damned villains, who did not guard her and keep her safe, and did not defend her sacred person from her foes!

"Sun, could you shine, and see my love beset, and yet not clothe your clouds in fiery coats, over all the heavens, with winged sulfurous flames, as when your beams, like mounted combatants, battled with the dragon Python in the uncultivated fields?"

Llewelyn wished that the Sun had protected his wife, Lady Eleanor, by destroying her enemies the way that Apollo the Sun-god had destroyed the dragon Python. In Llewelyn's version of the myth, Apollo destroyed Python by using the heat of the Sun.

Llewelyn continued, "But if kind Cambria — Wales — deign to give me good fortune and make me the chief Brute — King — of western Wales, I'll shorten that gain-legged Longshanks by the top by cutting off his head, and make his flesh my murdering falchion's food."

Longshanks was "gain-legged" because his long legs covered much territory with each step.

A falchion is a kind of sword.

Llewelyn continued, "To arms, true Britons, descended from the Trojans' seed, and with your swords write in the Book of Time your British names in letters of blood!"

The Book of Time is the metaphorical record of great events of history.

Llewelyn continued, "Owen ap Rice, while we wait for reinforcements, prepare, go away quickly on horseback, and take with you a hundred men chosen from your countrymen, and scour and ravage the marches — the borderlands between Wales and England — with your Welshmen's hooked weapons, so that Englishmen may think that the devil has come."

Llewelyn then said, "Rice ap Meredith shall remain with me. Make good use of your staying here to form a resolution to revenge these wrongs with the blood of thousands of men who are guiltless and innocent of this outrage. Fly on them with all speed!

"Edward, may my love — Lady Eleanor — be the ruin of your life!

"Follow me, countrymen! Words make no way: They do no work. My Lady Eleanor has been ambushed and captured. I am robbed of the comfort of my life. And I know this, and yet I am not avenged against him?"

Llewelyn and the other lords exited.

Friar Hugh ap David, Jack the novice, Guenthian, and Morgan Pigot the harper reentered the scene.

Friar Hugh ap David said to Jack the novice, "Come, boy, we must buckle on our swords, I see. The Prince of Wales has the same opinion as I. Rather than lose his wench, he will fight *ab ouo usque ad mala.*"

Ab ouo usque ad mala is Latin for "from the egg to the apple." It referred to the first course and last course of a Roman feast and means here metaphorically from the beginning to the end, or all the way to the end.

Jack the novice said, "Oh, master, don't doubt that your novice will prove to be a hot shot, with a bottle of metheglin."

Guenthian began to sing a Welsh song, Jack the novice sang the chorus, and then Friar Hugh ap David sang the finishing verses.

CHAPTER 3

— SCENE III —

At Berwick Castle, Berwick, on the border of England and Scotland, several people met to decide who would be King of Scotland following the unexpected death of King Alexander III.

The nine lords of Scotland (including John Baliol) who were competing to be King were present, along with their pages.

Also present were the Earl of Gloucester, the Earl of Sussex, King Edward in his suit of glass, Queen Eleanor, the Queen-Mother, and Joan.

Edward's suit of glass was a robe decorated with small diamond-shaped pieces of reflective glass. The pieces of reflective glass acted like — or were — small mirrors.

The King and Queen of England were under a canopy.

King Edward I said, "Nobles of Scotland, we thank you all for the gentle princely service you have done this day to Edward, England's King and Scotland's lord."

The Kings of England in this era regarded themselves as Scotland's feudal overlords.

King Edward I continued, "Our coronation's due ceremony has ended with the applause of all ranks of people. Now, then, let us repose and rest us here. But especially we thank you, gentle lords, because you so well have governed your griefs, as, being grown unto a general quarrel, you choose King Edward by your messengers, to calm, to qualify, and to settle the enkindled strife of Scotland's climbing peers."

After the Scottish King Alexander III died, several Scottish nobles wanted to become the next King of Scotland. Such a situation can lead to civil war. To avoid that evil, the nobles asked King Edward I of England to decide who shall become the next King of Scotland.

King Edward I continued, "I have no doubt, fair lords, but you well know how factions waste the richest commonwealth, and you well know how discord spoils the seats of mighty Kings."

He then mentioned the rebellion of the nobles against his father, King Henry III, in the Second Barons' War: "The Barons' War, a tragic wicked war, nobles, how it has shaken England's strength!"

King Edward I continued, "Industriously, it seems to me, you have loyally ventured to prevent this shock."

They had avoided civil war by allowing King Edward I to choose which of the nine lords of Scotland would be the next King of Scotland.

King Edward I continued, "Since you have chosen me to be your judge, my lords, I ask you if you will accept the decision I will make regarding who shall be your King?"

Baliol said, "Victorious Edward, to whom the Scottish Kings owe homage — public respect and honor — as their lord and sovereign, among us nine lords there is only one lawful King."

His words acknowledged King Edward I as overlord of Scotland.

Baliol continued, "But if we nine were all to be judges in the case, then in Scotland there would be nine Kings at once because each of the nine judges would choose himself to be King — this contention between we nine lords would never be settled by the selection of nine persons to be King.

"To prevent these quarrels, we nine Scottish lords jointly make an appeal to your imperial throne, who knows our claims to be the next King of Scotland. We stand not on our titles before your grace, but instead we submit ourselves to your award. And to whomever your majesty shall name to be our King, we'll yield our obedience to him as our King. Thus willingly, and of their own accord, do the nobles of Scotland make great England's King Edward Scotland's judge."

Using the royal plural, King Edward I said, "Then, nobles, since you all agree as one to this judgment about a crown you all disagree about whom shall wear, and since what judgment I make shall be unappealable, hold up your hands in the sight of all of you, and with one general voice, state that you are content to accept our decision and obey the man we select to be King of Scotland."

All nine nobles held up their hands and said, "He shall decide who shall be our King."

King Edward I said, "Give me the golden diadem."

This was the crown of the King of Scotland.

He held up the crown and said, "Look, here I hold the goal for which you strived, and here behold it, my worthy Scottish men-at-arms, all of whom for chivalry and worthy wisdom's praise are worthy each one of you to wear a diadem.

"Expect my judgment, as formerly at Mount Ida's foothills the divine goddesses awaited the award of Dardan's son."

He was referring to the famous Judgment of Paris. Three goddesses — Juno, Venus, and Minerva — argued over who was the most beautiful, so they got Paris, a Prince of Troy and descendant of the King named Dardanus, to decide who was the most beautiful.

King Edward I said, "Baliol, step forward."

He gave Baliol the crown and said, "Baliol, behold, I give you the Scottish crown. Wear it with heart and with thankfulness.

"Sound trumpets, and say all after me, God save King Baliol, the Scottish King!"

The trumpets sounded, and all cried aloud, "God save King Baliol, the Scottish King."

King Edward I said, "Thus, lords, although you require no reason why, it is according to the conscience in the cause that I make John Baliol your anointed King.

"Honor and love him, as best suits the man who is in peace possessed of Scotland's crown."

Adopting the royal plural, Baliol said, "Thanks, royal King of England, for your honor done to us. This justice that has calmed our civil strife shall now be ceased with honorable love.

"So moved by remorse and pity are we that we will erect a college of my name. In Oxford I will build Baliol College to ensure the memory of Baliol's generosity and his gratitude.

"And let me have happy days only as long as I shall be loyal to England."

Queen Eleanor said, "Now, brave John Baliol, Lord of Galloway and King of Scots, shine with your golden-crowned head. Shake your spears, in honor of his name — Edward — under whose royalty you wear the same."

King Edward I said, "And, lovely King of England, to your lovely Queen, lovely Queen Eleanor, to her turn your eye, whose honor cannot but love you well."

Queen Eleanor now made a long speech in praise of her husband:

"The sky, spangled throughout with the golden spots that are the stars, reflects no finer sight in a frosty night than lovely Longshanks in his Eleanor's eye.

"So, Ned, your Nell is in every part of you, your body is garded — adorned — and guarded with a troop of Queens, and every Queen is as brave and splendid as Eleanor."

Queen Eleanor was reflected in the diamond-shaped pieces of glass adorning his robe. Those pieces of reflective glass were called quarries and orbes.

Queen Eleanor continued, "Each of these reflected Queens gives glory to these glorious crystal quarries, where every orbe entertains an object — a Queen — of rich device and princely majesty.

"Thus like Narcissus, diving in the deep, I die in honor and in the King of England's arms; and if I drown, it is in my delight."

In this culture, "to die" can mean "to have an orgasm."

Narcissus is a mythological man who fell in love with his own reflection in a pool of water.

Queen Eleanor continued, "Your company is the chief life in death, from forth whose coral — red — lips I suck the sweetness with which are made dainty Cupid's caudles."

Cupid is the son of Venus, and he is the god of love.

Caudles are medicinal drinks.

Queen Eleanor continued, "Then live or die, brave Ned, either sink or swim.

"An earthly bliss it is to look on him.

"On you, sweet Ned, it shall befit your Nell to be bounteous — generous — to the beauteous people.

"Look over the tops of the palm trees, sweet fountains of my bliss,

"And I will stand on tiptoe for a kiss."

The "sweet fountains of my bliss" were Edward's eyes.

King Edward I replied to Queen Eleanor:

"He [Any man] had no thought of any gentle heart,

"Who would not seize desire for such desart [desert]

"If any heavenly joy in women be,

"Sweet of all sweets, sweet Nell, it is in thee [you]."

He then returned to business:

"Now, lords, let's go.

"By this time, the Earl of March, Lord Mortimer, has stationed his men over Cambria's mountain-tops, and feels Llewelyn's mind. He wants to know what Llewelyn is planning."

Lord Mortimer, who had much land in Wales, was an enemy to Llewelyn.

Using the royal plural, King Edward I continued, "To which territory, which Llewelyn's men have been ravaging, now that our solemn service of coronation is past, we will swiftly travel to back up our friends as needed.

"And into Wales our men-at-arms shall march, and we shall march with them in person, foot by foot."

He then said to Baliol, King of Scotland, "Brother of Scotland, you shall go to your home and at the coronation you shall meet your loving peers and live in honor there as the fair friend of the King of England."

He continued speaking to others:

"And thou, sweet Nell, Queen of King Edward's heart, shall now come lesser at your dainty love — we shall be separated because of war — until storms are past, and we have cooled the rage of these rebellious Welshmen who contend against England's majesty and Edward's crown.

"Sound, trumpets!

"Heralds, lead the train of nobles along.

"This is King Edward's feast and holiday."

Later, in London, Queen Eleanor, Joan, and the Earl of Gloucester stood together on a street in front of the palace.

A band of musicians played as the Mayoress — the wife of the Mayor of London — returned from church. The Mayoress' name was Mary.

Queen Eleanor said, "Gloucester, who may this person be? A bride or what?

"Please, Joan, go see,

"And learn the reason for the harmony."

Joan went to the Mayoress and brought her over to Queen Eleanor.

Joan said to the Mayoress, "Good woman, let it not offend you any in the least to deliver to me the reason why in this unusual manner you pass the streets with music ceremoniously."

The Mayoress was uncertain of Joan's rank. If she ranked higher than the Mayoress, then the Mayoress should call her "madam"; if of lower rank, she should call her "mistress."

She said to Joan, "Mistress, or madam, whichever you are, know that I am the Mayor of London's wife, who has given birth to a son, which I have not done for the previous dozen years.

"Now in my husband's year of being the Mayor of London, bringing him a splendid boy, I pass to my house as if I were a maiden bride — a newlywed.

"This private pleasure of mine, something that God approves of, shall here in no way, I hope, offend good people."

Queen Eleanor said:

"You hope so, gentle mistress. Do you indeed?

"But do not make it part of your creed."

A creed is a statement of belief. The Mayoress hoped that the Queen was not offended, but the Queen was offended — capriciously, without reason.

The Mayoress thought, *Alas, I am ruined! She is the Queen — the proudest Queen whom England ever knew.*

The Mayoress and the musicians exited.

Queen Eleanor said, "Come, Gloucester, let's go to the court and revel there."

CHAPTER 4

— SCENE IV —

The English army was now nearing Carnarvon Castle in northwest Wales.

Llewelyn and Rice ap Meredith were standing outside the castle. Sir David, Llewelyn's spy and brother, had stolen away from the English army and was approaching the castle.

Seeing Sir David, Rice ap Meredith drew his sword.

Sir David said, "Wait! Isn't it Meredith I see?"

Recognizing his brother, Llewelyn said, "All is well; we are all friends.

"Meredith, see the man who must and will make us great, and who will raise Llewelyn's head so that it wears the crown of the King of England.

"Fight, Llewelyn, for your friends and yourself."

Rice ap Meredith said, "Fight — despite strong fortune, our army's strong — and sweep away your foes before your pointed lance."

Sir David said, "Not too much prowess, my good lord, at once. Let's have some talk of policy another while."

He wanted to talk about strategy in the deployment of that army later. Right now, he had intelligence to deliver to Llewelyn.

Rice ap Meredith asked, "How come your limbs hurt at this assault?"

He thought that Sir David was hesitant about Llewelyn's army attacking Edward I's army.

Llewelyn said, "Sir David's limbs hurt for our good, Meredith. Take note of that."

He was assuring Rice ap Meredith that Sir David was loyal.

Llewelyn said, "Sir David's intelligence is full of good ideas, and he properly will perform what he says he will perform."

"Enough of this, my lord, at once," Sir David said. "What do you want me to do, now that I am friendly with King Edward I and he trusts me?

"What shall I especially advise King Edward and the English lords as I am sitting in council? What counsel should I give so that I may help my Welsh friends?"

Llewelyn said, "David, if you will best for me give counsel, advise the English that my love — Lady Eleanor, daughter of Simon de Montfort — should be rendered to my hand.

"Tell them that neither the chains that Mulciber formerly made to tie Prometheus' limbs to the mountain in the Caucasus, nor Furies' fangs shall keep me long from her, but I will take her from the usurper's tent."

Prometheus stole fire from the gods and gave it to humans. Mulciber (which means "fire allayer" and is another name for Vulcan, the blacksmith god) punished him by chaining him to a boulder in one of the mountains in the Caucasus mountain range.

The Furies are goddesses of vengeance.

Llewelyn continued, "My beauteous Lady Eleanor!

"David, if your intelligence may help your friends in anything in this case, express it, then, in this, and in nothing else. Come up with a plan that will deliver Lady Eleanor, my wife, to me."

Sir David said, "Aye, there's a card that puts us to our trump."

King Edward I's capture of Lady Eleanor was forcing the Welsh to play their trump cards.

Sir David continued, "For if I could see the star of Leicester's loins, it would be enough to darken and obscure King Edward's glory, fortune, and pride."

Lady Eleanor was "the star of Leicester's loins." Her father was the Earl of Leicester: Simon de Montfort.

Sir David continued, "First, here is something that I can put you out of doubt: Lord Mortimer of the King has her in his charge, and he honorably treats your Lady Eleanor.

"Some think he prays that Llewelyn were in Heaven, for if that happens, he hopes to couch his love on earth."

Some people think that Lord Mortimer would love to have and couch (that is, lay horizontally) Lady Eleanor.

Llewelyn said, "No, that will not happen. Where Llewelyn mounts, there Ellen flies. Ineffable are my thoughts for her: She is not from me in death to be divorced.

"Go on, tell us your plan. It shall be done, whatever it shall be.

"Edward is completely convinced that you are loyal to him. So are all the English lords and barons. So then what can prevent you from intruding on them some newfound strategy to test their intelligence and fool them?"

Sir David said, "I have an idea.

"Meredith, take my weapons.

"I am your prisoner. At least, Llewelyn, you will say that I am your prisoner. Go from here, and when you parle on the walls, make a pretense of monstrous tyranny that you say you intend to execute on me, as on the man who shamefully rebels against kin and kind — family and human nature.

"Say that unless you will have your love, Lady Eleanor, you will execute me. Then make your peace with such conditions as shall best concern you.

"Say that David must die a shameful death. Edward, perhaps, moved by mercy and pity, will in exchange yield Lady Eleanor to you, and you through me shall gain your heart's desire."

Llewelyn said, "This is sweetly advised. David, you bless me, my brother David, lengthener of my life!

"Friends, congratulate me on my joyful hopes."

CHAPTER 5

Before Carnarvon Castle in Wales, King Edward I, the Earl of Sussex, Lord Mortimer, and others stood. They had been fighting the Welsh rebels, and King Edward I wanted the assault to continue.

King Edward I said, "Why, barons, do you allow our foes to rest and catch their breath? Assault, assault, and charge them with all speed!

"They fear, they flee, they faint, they fight in vain.

"But where is gentle Sir David? In his den? I am loath that anything but good should happen to him."

A trumpet sounded.

On the walls of the castle, Llewelyn, Friar Hugh ap David, and some soldiers appeared. Rice ap Meredith, who had a dagger in his hand, also appeared, holding Sir David by the collar.

King Edward I said loudly, "Where is the proud disturber of our state, traitor to Wales and to his sovereign?"

Llewelyn replied, "Usurper, here I am. What do thou want?"

King Edward I replied, "Welshman, I want allegiance, which thou owe your King."

They were calling each other "thou" instead of the respectful "you."

Llewelyn responded, "Thou are a traitor and no King — thou seek your country's sack and despoilation. Thou are the famous runagate of Christendom."

The word "runagate" means "vagabond" and also "apostate" (one who has renounced his religion) — a cutting insult to King Edward I, who had recently returned from a Crusade.

"Ambitious rebel, do thou know who I am, and how great, how famous, and how fortunate I am?" King Edward I replied. "And do thou dare carry arms against me here, even when thou should do reverence at my feet? Yes, feared and honored in the farthest parts has Edward, the noble Henry's son, been.

"Traitor, this sword unsheathed has often been shined while reeking — steaming — with the blood of Saracens."

King Edward I was saying that he had often shined his sword by stabbing Muslims with it.

He continued, "Similar to Perseus on Pegasus, his winged steed, brandishing bright the sword-blade of adamant that aged Saturn gave fair Maia's son, while fighting with Medusa the Gorgon in the valley, I set my army on the Muslims before the gates of Nazareth and stained my horse's hooves in pagans' gore, sending whole centuries of heathen souls to Pluto's house."

Adamant is a very hard mineral.

Saturn was the father of many of the Olympian gods, including Jupiter and Juno.

Maia is the mother of Mercury.

The word "century" is a Roman military term. A Roman century is a unit of one hundred soldiers.

Pluto is the god of the Land of the Dead.

King Edward I continued, "This sword, this bloodthirsty sword, aims at your head, and shall, I hope, before long, measure and divide your bowels and your belly, disloyal villain, thou, and who is more —"

He was going to say "more disloyal than thou," but Llewelyn interrupted him.

Llewelyn said, "Why, Longshanks, do thou think I will be scared with words? No. Even if thou spoke in thunder like Jove, or even if thou would, like the monstrous giant Briareus, shake at once a hundred bloody swords with a hundred bloody hands, I tell you, Longshanks, here is a man — me — who faces you whom nothing can daunt, no, not even the stroke of death.

"I am resolved, as you can see, but see here and now the chance of war."

He pointed to Sir David and said, "Do thou know a traitor if thou see his head? Then, Longshanks, look this villain in the face. This rebel has wrought his country's wrack and ruin. He is a base rascal; he is bad in his character and hated because of his character. He is an object of wrath, and he is the subject of revenge."

King Edward I said, "Llewelyn, do thou call this the chance of war? This is bad for us all, pardie, but worse for him."

"Pardie" is "*par Dieu,*" which is French for "by God."

King Edward I then said, "Courage, Sir David! Thou know Kings must die, and noble minds defy all dastardly, cowardly fear."

Sir David said, "Renowned Edward, star of England's globe, my dearest lord and sweetest sovereign, glorious and happy is this chance occurrence to me, which allows me to reap this fame and honor in my death because I was hewed with foul defiled hands for my beloved King and country's good and died in grace and favor with my Prince."

He then said to his "captors," whose side he was really on, "Seize on me, bloody butchers, with your paws. It is only temporal, earthly harm that you can inflict on me."

Religious people believe that the glories of Heaven vastly outweigh any and all temporal evils we suffer on Earth.

King Edward I said to Sir David, "Bravely resolved, brave soldier, by my life!"

Friar Hugh ap David, standing beside Sir David, said to him, "Pay attention, sir, I am afraid that you will not be so resolved by that time you know what I can show you. Here there are hot dogs, I can tell you, that mean to have the tormenting of you."

"Dogs" are pincers, and "hot dogs" are red-hot pincers. They are instruments of torture.

Lord Mortimer said, "Llewelyn, in the midst of all your blustering threats, how will thou treat your brother whom thou have captured? Will thou let his master ransom him?"

Llewelyn said, "No, nor will I allow his mistress, gallant Mortimer, to ransom him with all the gold and silver of the land."

Rice ap Meredith said, "Ransom this Judas — this traitor — to his father's line! Ransom this traitor to his brother's life! No."

He then said to Sir David, "Take this earnest-penny of your death."

He seemed to cut Sir David's arms and shoulders — these were not mortal wounds. An "earnest-penny" is a small down payment of a larger amount of money to come.

Rice ap Meredith continued, "This touch, my lord, comes nothing near the mark."

The mark is the target — the target is a part of Sir David's body, such as the heart — that would result in his death.

King Edward I said, "Oh, damned villain, hold your hands! Stop torturing Sir David! Ask and have."

This meant: "Ask for what you want as a ransom, and you shall have it."

Llewelyn responded, "We will not ask nor have. Do thou see these tools?"

Llewelyn showed King Edward I red-hot pincers and said, "These are the dogs — the pincers — that shall torture him to death. They shall tear his cursed flesh into pieces, and here in your sight he shall hang and suffer."

King Edward I said, "Oh, villains! Traitors, how I will get Sir David avenged!"

Llewelyn said, "What! Do thou threaten us, Edward? Reckless minds scorn that which fury menaces."

He then said, "See the effect your words have on me."

He seemed to cut Sir David's nose.

Sir David cried, "Oh, gracious heavens, dissolve me back into the clay my body came from! This tyranny is more than flesh can bear."

King Edward I said, "Bear it, brave mind, since nothing but your blood may satisfy in these extreme circumstances."

The Earl of Sussex said to King Edward I, "My lord, it is in vain to threaten them. They are resolved, as you see, upon his death."

King Edward I replied, "Sussex, they all shall pay dearly for the death of Sir David. Offer them anything for his life — pardon, or peace, or anything else. May God love me as much as I love my friends!"

He then said, "Llewelyn, let me have your brother's life even at what expense and ransom thou will name."

Llewelyn responded, "Edward — King Edward, as thou wish to be termed — thou know that thou have my beauteous Lady Eleanor as your captive. Produce her here and now to plead for David's life. She may obtain more than an army of men can obtain."

King Edward I replied, "Will thou exchange your prisoner — Sir David — for your love — Lady Eleanor?"

"Talk no more to me," Llewelyn said. "Let me see her face."

Mortimer said, "Why, will your majesty be all so low and base that you stoop to his demands in everything?"

King Edward I said, "Fetch Lady Eleanor at once. Good Mortimer, go now."

Mortimer said to himself, "I go; but how unwillingly Heaven does know."

He was in love with Lady Eleanor.

Rice ap Meredith said, "Hurry, Mortimer, if thou love your friend."

Mortimer said to himself, "I go for dearer than I leave behind."

He valued Lady Eleanor more than he valued Sir David.

He exited.

King Edward I said, "See, Sussex, Sir David bleeds within my eyesight. He bears bad fortune's shock triumphantly."

Friar Hugh ap David said to Llewelyn, "Sa-ha, master! I have found something! I have found something!"

"Sa-ha" was a hunting cry that announced a discovery of something, such as signs of the prey that the hunters were hunting.

Llewelyn asked, "What have thou found, Friar?"

Rice ap Meredith answered:

"News, my lord, a star from out the sea;

"The same is risen and made a summer's day."

This was a poetic way of saying that Lady Eleanor had been sighted. She was compared to the Sun rising over the sea in the summer.

Lord Mortimer returned, leading Lady Eleanor.

Seeing Lady Eleanor and Lord Mortimer, Llewelyn said, "What, Nell, sweet Nell, do I see your face?

"Let the heavens fall, let the stars flee, let Phoebus' lamp — the Sun — shine no more!

"This is the heavenly body that lends this world her light. This is the star of my fortune, this star that shines so brightly. This is the Queen of my heart, the loadstar — the guiding light — of my delight, this fair manifestation of beauty, this miracle of fame!

"Oh, let me die with Lady Eleanor in my arms!"

In this culture, "to die" can mean "to have an orgasm."

Llewelyn continued, "What honor shall I lend your loyalty or what praise shall I lend to your sacred godhead?"

Rice ap Meredith said, "By the Virgin Mary, the answer is this, my lord, if I may give you counsel: Sacrifice this mongrel, her friend, in her sight."

He meant that Lord Mortimer should be sacrificed to honor her.

In this culture, the word "friend" could mean "lover."

Rice ap Meredith continued, "Once this sacrifice is done, one of your soldiers may dip his foul shirt in Mortimer's blood. If you do this, you shall be waited on by as many crosses as King Edward."

King Edward I's crusading soldiers wore crosses on their coats. Rice ap Meredith meant that the death of Lord Mortimer — a major enemy of the Welsh — would result in many soldiers joining the cause of the Welsh rebels.

King Edward I said, "Maintain good cheer, Sir David; we shall be up on the walls of the castle soon."

Lord Mortimer said to himself, "Die, Mortimer; your life is almost gone."

He felt that he would die if his beloved — Lady Eleanor — were given to Llewelyn.

Lady Eleanor said to Llewelyn, "Sweet Prince of Wales, if I were within your arms, then I would in peace possess my love, and the heavens would open their fair crystal gates so that I may see the palace of my intent."

To Lady Eleanor, being in Llewelyn's arms would be like entering Heaven.

"Llewelyn, set your brother free," King Edward I said. "Let me have Sir David, and thou shall have Lady Eleanor."

Llewelyn said, "Truly, Edward, I prize my Lady Eleanor more dearly than I prize my life; but there belongs more to these affairs than my happiness in love: And to be short, if thou will have your man, whom, I swear, thou over-value, then the safety of Llewelyn and his men must be highly considered in this coming to terms.

"Say, therefore, and be short and quick, will thou give peace and pardon to Llewelyn and his men?"

King Edward I said, "I will need time to seek advice before making a decision."

Llewelyn said, "King Edward, no. We will permit no pause — if there is a pause, then this wretch, this traitor, goes into the cooking pot."

This idiom meant that Sir David would be killed.

Using the royal plural, Llewelyn continued, "And if Llewelyn is pursued so closely by your soldiers, Llewelyn may by some chance show you such a tumbling-cast, as formerly our father suffered when he thought to escape from Julius Caesar's tower but broke his neck instead."

If King Edward I would not make peace with and give pardons to Llewelyn and the other Welsh rebels, they would throw Sir David down from the castle wall.

Julius Caesar's tower was the Tower of London, which the English believed that he had built.

Llewelyn's father had been held prisoner in the Tower of London, but he fell to his death during an escape attempt.

The Earl of Sussex said, "My lord, these rebels are all desperate."

Lord Mortimer said to himself, "And Mortimer is of all men the most miserable."

King Edward I said to Llewelyn's soldiers, "What do you say, Welshmen? Will you leave your arms — your weapons — and be true and loyal liegemen to Edward's crown?"

The First Welsh Soldier said, "If Edward will pardon absolutely what is past, upon some conditions we will all be content."

King Edward I said drily, "It's likely that you will require some conditions from us, then?"

A common soldier was negotiating with a King. Unusual.

The First Welsh Soldier said, "We have special conditions for our safety first, and also for our country Cambria's common good, to avoid the effusion of our guilty blood."

Understandably, the Welsh soldiers wanted to ensure that they and their country would be safe.

"Go on," King Edward I said. "Continue to speak."

The First Welsh Soldier said, "First, for our followers, and ourselves, and all, we ask for a pardon in the King's word.

"Then we ask for this lord's — Llewelyn's — possession of his love: Lady Eleanor.

"But we beg these boons for our country's chief, and we beg England's princely promise to your Wales: Promise that no one will be Cambria's Prince to govern us except he who is a Welshman, born in Wales. We want none other than Welshmen to be the chief of Wales.

"Grant this, and swear it on your knightly sword, and you will have your man and us and all in peace."

"Have your man" was ambiguous. The First Welsh Soldier meant that King Edward I would have Sir David returned to him, but Llewelyn thought that the soldier was referring to him.

Llewelyn said, "Why, Cambria-Britons, are you so incensed against me? Will you deliver me into Edward's hands?"

The First Welsh Soldier replied, "No, Lord Llewelyn. We will back you up so that you have your life, your love, and golden liberty."

Mortimer said to himself, "A truce with honorable conditions taken. This means Wales' happiness, England's glory, and my poison."

It was his poison because Lady Eleanor would be given to Llewelyn.

King Edward I ordered, "Command that retreat be sounded in our camp."

He said to the Welsh soldiers, "Soldiers, I grant in full what you request."

He then said, "David, have good cheer.

"Llewelyn, open the gates."

Using the respectful "you," Llewelyn replied, "The gates are opened. You and yours may enter."

Sir David said, "The sweetest Sun that ever I saw to shine!"

King Edward I said to Lady Eleanor, "Madam, this was a quarrel well begun for you. Be my guest and Sir Llewelyn's love."

Everyone exited except Lord Mortimer.

He said to himself, "Mortimer, this was a brabble ill begun for you. It is a truce containing capital conditions: A prisoner was saved and ransomed with your life."

The capital conditions meant his death: Without Lady Eleanor, he felt that he would die.

He continued, "Edward, my King, my lord, and dear friend, very little do you know how this retreat, as with a sword, has slain poor Mortimer.

"Farewell the flower, the gem of beauty's blaze, sweet Ellen, miracle of nature's hand!

"Hell is in your name, but Heaven is in your looks."

Ellen is a part of Eleanor's name. So is *'ell.*

Lord Mortimer continued:

"Sweet Venus, let me saint or devil be

"In that sweet Heaven or Hell that is in thee."

Venus is the goddess of love and sexual passion.

CHAPTER 6

At Carnarvon Castle, Wales, Jack the novice and Morgan Pigot the harper found standing places from which to view the Queen as they waited for the arrival of Queen Eleanor.

The trumpets sounded.

Queen Eleanor entered the scene, riding in her litter borne by four black North Africans.

With her were Joan of Acre, Katherine (her attendant), and other ladies.

Her attendants included the Earl of Gloucester and her four footmen. One set a ladder against the side of the litter. Queen Eleanor descended, and her daughter followed her.

"Give me my slippers," Queen Eleanor said. "Bah, this hot weather — how it makes me sweat! Heigh-ho, my heart!"

"Heigh-ho" indicated fatigue.

She continued, "Bah, I am exceedingly faint! Give me my fan so that I may cool my face. Wait, take my mask, but see that you don't rumple it."

In this culture, upper-class ladies wore masks to protect their faces from the Sun and weather.

Queen Eleanor continued, "This wind and dust, see how it smolders me!"

"Give me something to drink, good Gloucester, or I will die for lack of something to drink!"

King Edward was not present, but she addressed him in an apostrophe:

"Ah, Ned, you have forgotten your Nell I see,

"Because she is thus forced to follow thee!"

Queen Eleanor was heavily pregnant, but she was obeying his orders to come to Wales. He had promised the Welsh soldiers that only a person born in Wales would be the chief Welshman and rule Wales. Therefore, he hoped that Queen Eleanor would give birth to a boy in Wales.

The Earl of Gloucester said to her, "This air's heat, if it please your majesty, harmful and noxious through mountains' vapors and thick mist, must be unpleasant to you and your company, you who never were accustomed to take the air until Flora, goddess of gardens and flowers, has perfumed the earth with sweet scents, with lilies, roses, mints, and eglantine."

"Eglantine" is the species of rose known as the sweet-briar.

Queen Eleanor replied, "I tell you, the ground is entirely too base for Eleanor to honor with her steps. Eleanor's footpace, when she travelled in the streets of Acre and the fair Jerusalem, was upon nothing except costly arras-points, fair island-tapestry, and azured — blue — silk."

In such places as Acre (where her daughter Joan was born) and Jerusalem, she stepped on nothing except rich tapestries and carpeting and silk.

Queen Eleanor continued, "My milk-white steed tread on striped cloth and trampled proudly underneath its feet the choicest of our English woolen fabrics."

Aeschylus' play *Agamemnon* shows the leader of the Greeks against the Trojans in the Trojan War tramping underfoot and ruining a rich cloth that his adulterous wife, Clytemnestra, had laid on the ground. This act showed his overweening pride.

She continued, "This climate frowning with black congealed clouds that take their swelling and growing from the marshy soil, fraught with infectious fogs and misty damps, is far too unworthy to be once embalmed with the redolence of this refreshing breath of mine, which sweetens wherever it alights, as do the flames and holy fires of Vesta's sacrifice."

This culture regarded fogs and air from marshes as dangerous.

Joan, Queen Eleanor's daughter, began to praise the air of England: "The pleasant fields of England newly planted with the spring, make Thamesis mount above its banks, and, like a pleasant person, wallow up and down on Flora's beds and Napae's silver down."

"Thamesis" is the Latinized name of the Thames River.

Flora is the goddess of gardens and flowers.

Napae are nymphs who live in wooded valleys.

At this time, "down" could mean hills and mountains.

Gloucester said to Joan, whom he was courting:

"And Wales is the same for me, madam, while you are here.

"No climate is good unless your grace is near.

"I wish that Wales had something that could please you half so well or I — Gloucester — had any precious thing that your ladyship could demand that I give to you."

"Well said, my lord!" Joan said, "It is as my mother says: You men have learned to woo a thousand ways."

Queen Eleanor was well aware that Gloucester wanted to marry Joan. So was Joan.

Gloucester said, "Oh, madam, had I learned, in case of need, out of all those ways to woo, one way to speed and succeed, my cunning, then, had been my fortune's guide."

He wanted to know just one way to court Joan that would lead to their being married.

Queen Eleanor said, "Truly, Joan, I think you must be Gloucester's bride."

She thought:

The good Earl of Gloucester, how close he steps to her side!

So soon this eye these younglings had espied.

Apparently, the Earl of Gloucester had early and easily fallen in love with Joan, and Queen Eleanor had early and easily learned of his love for Joan and of Joan's love for him.

Queen Eleanor continued speaking to Joan: "I'll tell you, girl, when I was fair and young, I found such honey in sweet Edward's tongue that I could never spend one idle walk with Ned, but he and I would lengthen it with our conversation."

She then said to the Earl of Gloucester:

"So will you, my lord, when you have got your Joan.

"No matter, let Queen-mother be alone.

"Old Nell is mother now, and grandmother may be soon."

"Queen-mother" and "Old Nell" referred to Queen Eleanor herself. Joan would leave her to marry and live with Gloucester, and likely Queen Eleanor would become a grandmother due to Joan's having a baby with Gloucester. Also, Queen Eleanor was soon to give birth.

Queen Eleanor continued:

"The greenest grass does droop and turn to hay.

"Woo on, kind scholar, good Gloucester, love your Joan.

"Her heart is yours, her eyes are not her own."

Joan's eyes were not her own because they were constantly looking at Gloucester.

Gloucester said, "This comfort, madam, that your grace gives me binds me in double duty while I live."

He will have his duty to the King and Queen and England, and also to Joan.

He continued, "I wish to God that King Edward will see and say no less!"

Gloucester was grateful for the Queen's blessing, and he hoped to be grateful for the King's blessing.

Queen Eleanor said, "Gloucester, I assure you upon my life that my King is pleased to give you his daughter for your wife.

"Sweet Ned has not forgotten, since he did woo,

"The gall of love and all that belongs thereto."

"Gall" is bitterness. Love has its sweetness but also sometimes its bitterness.

Gloucester asked, "Why, was your grace so shy to one so kind?"

Queen Eleanor replied, "Kind, Gloucester! So, I think, indeed, it seems he loves his wife no more than is necessary, he who sent for us in all speedy haste, knowing his Queen to be so great with child, and made me leave my princely pleasant seats to come into his ruder part of Wales."

She was angry at her husband for forcing her to make a long and difficult journey while she was heavily pregnant.

Gloucester said, "His highness has some secret reason why he wishes you to move from England's pleasant court.

"The Welshmen have for a long time been asking that when the war of the rebels reaches an end, none might be Prince and ruler over them but such a person who is their countryman. This suit, I think, his grace has granted them."

If only a person born in Wales could rule over the Welsh, King Edward I wanted his son — if Queen Eleanor were to give birth to a boy — to be born in Wales.

Queen Eleanor said, "So, then, it is King Edward's policy to have his son — indeed, if it should be a son — a Welshman. Well, a Welsh son pleases me. And here the King comes."

King Edward I and his lords entered the scene.

King Edward I said, "Nell, welcome into Wales! How fares my Eleanor? How are you?"

"Never worse!" Queen Eleanor said. "Curse their hearts! It is a long journey."

King Edward replied, "Hearts, sweet Nell?

"Curse no hearts where such sweet saints do dwell."

He held her hand tightly.

Queen Eleanor said, "Nay, then, I see I have my dream. Please let go."

King Edward I did not let go of her hand.

"You will not let go, will you, whether I want you to hold my hand or not?" Queen Eleanor said. "You are disposed to make me angry."

King Edward I replied, "Say anything but that. Once, Nell, you gave me this hand."

"Please, let go," Queen Eleanor requested. "You are inclined to be merry and tease me, I think."

"Aye, madam, very well," King Edward I said.

Queen Eleanor said, "Let go and be hanged, I say!"

"What ails my Nell?" King Edward I asked.

Queen Eleanor said, "Ah, woe to me. What sudden fits are these I am experiencing? What grief, what pinching pain, like young men's love, that make me run like a madwoman thus hither and thither?"

Still holding her hand, King Edward I asked, "What! Are you melancholy, Nell?"

Queen Eleanor requested, "My lord, please, let go of me."

He let go of her hand.

She requested, "Give me fresh water. Why, how hot it is!"

Gloucester thought, *These be the fits that trouble men's wits.*

In other words, women can drive men crazy.

King Edward I said, "Joan, ask your beauteous mother how she is."

She was angry enough and ill enough that he was afraid to talk directly to her.

"How fares your majesty?" Joan asked her mother.

Queen Eleanor replied, "Joan, I am aggrieved at the heart, and angered worse because I cannot right me."

"Right me" can mean that she was so pregnant that she could not right herself and sit up straight after she leant too far to one side, but it could at the same time mean that as of yet, she cannot get her rights — rights such as not having her hand held when she does not want it held.

She continued, "I think the King comes purposely to spite me.

"My fingers itch until I have had my will:

Proud Edward, call in your Eleanor; be still.

"It will not be, nor rest I anywhere

"Until I have set it soundly on his ear."

Joan thought, *Is that what you want? To hit my father's ear! Then leave me out of it!*

Queen Eleanor said, "Bah, how I fret with grief!"

King Edward I said, "Come here, Joan. Do you know what ails my Queen?"

"Not I, my lord," Joan said, not wanting to tell her father what his wife wanted.

Then she relented: "She longs, I think, to give your grace a box on the ear."

King Edward I said, "Wench, if that is all, we'll 'ear it well."

He meant, using the royal plural, "We'll bear it well."

He then said to his wife, "What, all amort! All dejected! How does my dainty Nell? Look up at me, sweet love. Unkind! You won't kiss me even once? That isn't possible."

Queen Eleanor said, "My lord, I think you do this expressly to annoy me."

King Edward I begged, "Sweetheart, just one kiss."

"For God's sake, let me go," Queen Eleanor said.

The King had grabbed her again.

"Sweetheart, a kiss," King Edward I begged.

"What, whether I want to or not?" Queen Eleanor said. "You will not leave? Let me alone, I say."

King Edward I said, "I must be better chid."

He may have been intentionally provoking her into hitting him so she would get it out of her system and calm down.

Queen Eleanor said, "No? You will?"

She hit her husband on the ear and said, "Take that, then, lusty lord. Sir, stop when you are told to stop."

King Edward I said, "Why, so, this chare is chared. This business is over and done with."

A "chare" is a chore. "To chare" means "to accomplish a chore."

Gloucester said, "A good one, by the cross."

Queen Eleanor said, "No force, no harm."

She believed that she hadn't hit him hard enough to hurt.

King Edward I said, "Nothing is harmful that does my Eleanor any good."

He then said:

"Learn, lords, in preparation for when you become married men, to bow to women's yoke.

"And sturdy though you be, you may not stir for every stroke."

In other words, sometimes you just have to take it.

King Edward I then said, "Now, my sweet Nell, how does my Queen?"

Queen Eleanor replied, "She boasts that the mighty King of England has felt her fist and taken a blow basely at Eleanor's hand."

King Edward I said, "And boast she may, with my kind permission because she is shrewish and disdainful.

"Lack nothing, Nell, until you have brought your lord a lovely boy."

Because of her pregnancy, King Edward I had been indulging her.

Queen Eleanor said, "*Ven acà*. I am sick."

Ven acà is Spanish for "Come here."

She said to her attendant, "Good Katherina, please, be at hand."

Katherine said, "This sickness, I hope, will bring King Edward a jolly boy."

King Edward I said, "And, Katherine, whoever brings me that news shall not go empty-handed."

Any messenger who brought that particular good news would be rewarded.

CHAPTER 7

— SCENE VII —

The English had taken over Carnarvon Castle, and the Welshmen had gone to the mountain Mannock-deny in Wales.

Mortimer, Llewelyn, Rice ap Meredith, and Lady Eleanor were talking together.

Mortimer had delivered Lady Eleanor to Llewelyn, but he was delaying his departure because he wanted to be with Lady Eleanor as long as possible.

"Farewell, Llewelyn, with your loving Nell," Mortimer said.

"God-a-mercy, Mortimer," Llewelyn said, "and so farewell."

"God-a-mercy" means "thank you."

Mortimer appeared to leave, but he hid nearby to keep an eye on the others.

Rice ap Meredith said, "Farewell and be hanged, half Sinon's serpent brood."

In the Trojan War, Sinon was the lying Greek who was intentionally left behind with the Trojan Horse when the Greeks pretended to leave Troy. He convinced the Trojans to take the Horse inside their city by telling them that according to the gods Troy would never be conquered while the Horse was in the city. A Trojan priest named Laocoön opposed taking the Horse inside Troy, and the gods who opposed the Trojans sent two sea-snakes to kill Laocoön and his two sons. The Trojan Horse was hollow and filled with Greek warriors who came out of the Horse that night and let the Greek army into Troy.

Llewelyn said, "Speak good words, Sir Rice ap Meredith. Wrongs have the best remedy when taken with time, patience, and policy.

"But where is the Friar? Who can tell me?"

Friar Hugh ap David entered the scene and said:

"That I can, master, very well.

"And say, indeed, what has happened.

"Must we at once go to Heaven or Hell?"

Lady Eleanor said, "To Heaven, Friar! Friar, no, bah! Such heavy souls mount not so high."

Their souls were heavy with sin because they had rebelled against King Edward I.

Friar Hugh ap David lay on the ground and said:

"Then, Friar, lie down and die;

"And if any ask the reason why,

"Answer and say you cannot tell,

"Unless because you must go to Hell."

Lady Eleanor said:

"No, Friar, because you did rebel.

"Gentle Sir Rice ap Meredith, ring out your knell!"

Llewelyn said, "And Mannock-deny will toll your passing-bell."

Rice ap Meredith would ring the Friar's knell, and the mountain's echo would ring the Friar's passing-bell.

Both knells and passing-bells ring to announce a person's death or funeral. In this case, the two would be much the same — the ringing and its echo — because the Friar has just "died," and his "funeral" was being held.

Llewelyn continued:

"So, there lies a straw.

"And now to the law."

"To lay a straw" means "to stop talking about something."

The mock funeral was over, and Llewelyn now began to talk about what he and the others would do in the Welsh mountains.

Because he had just been to a "funeral," he started with a mock sermon:

"Masters and friends, we came naked into the world, and now we are turned naked out of the good towns into the wilderness.

"Let me see. By the Mass, I think we are a handsome commonwealth. We are a handful of good fellows, set a-Sunning to dog on — to follow — our own discretion. We can do whatever we want, including Sunning ourselves.

"What do you say, sirs? We are enough to keep a passage."

According to Llewelyn, they were a large enough body of armed men to keep an army from passing through a narrow passage in the mountains.

Llewelyn continued, "Will you be ruled by me? Will you follow me and follow my advice?

"We'll get tomorrow from Brecknock the *Book of Robin Hood*. The Friar, who is literate, shall instruct us in Robin's way of life, and we'll follow it here fairly and well.

"Since King Edward I has put us among the cards he is discarding, and, as it were, turned us with deuces and treys out of the deck, every man shall take his standing on Mannock-deny, and wander like irregulars — outcasts — up and down the wilderness.

"I'll be the Master of Misrule — I'll be Robin Hood, that's for sure."

In this society, the Master of Misrule presided over Christmas games.

Llewelyn continued, "Cousin Rice ap Meredith, you shall be Little John.

"And here's Friar David as fit as a die for Friar Tuck.

"Now, my sweet Nell, if you will make up the mess — be the fourth in a group of four — with a good heart for Maid Marian, and do well with Llewelyn under the green-wood trees, with as good a will as in the good towns, why, *plena est curia.*"

"*Plena est curia*" is Latin for "our company is now complete."

He was playing with words. "*In plena Curia*" means "in the full Court."

Lady Eleanor said, "My sweetest love, my infract — broken and unbroken — fortune could never boast her sovereignty."

Words change meaning over time, and "infract" can mean "broken" or "unbroken."

Lady Eleanor's fortune was broken in the sense that she was living in the wilderness and not in a court, but her fortune was unbroken in the sense that she was living with her husband, whom she loved.

She had given her sovereignty to her husband, and he ruled her.

She continued, "And if you should cross the ford of Phlegethon in the Land of the Dead—"

Phlegethon is a river of fire.

She continued, "— or swim the Hellespont with Leander —"

Leander swam the Hellespont, aka the Dardanelles, each night to be with Hero, the woman whom he loved. She lit a torch for him so he would swim in the right direction, but one night the wind blew the torch out and Leander drowned.

She continued, "— or in deserts forever dwell with Onophrius —"

Onophrius, a Catholic hermit, dwelt in the desert for seventy years.

She continued, "— or build your bower on Aetna's fiery tops —"

A bower is a home, and Aetna is Mount Etna, a volcano.

She concluded:

"Your Nell would follow you and keep with you,

"Your Nell would feed with you and sleep with you."

Friar Hugh ap David said, "*O Cupido quantus quantus*!"

The Latin means, "Oh, Cupid, how great! How great!"

Rice ap Meredith said, "Bravely resolved, madam."

He then asked, "And then what remains to do, my Lord Robin, but that we will live and die together like Camber-Britons — like Robin Hood, Little John, Friar Tuck, and Maid Marian?"

Llewelyn said, "There remains nothing to do now, cousin, but that I sell my gold chain to get money to dress us all in green, and we'll all play the diggers to make us a cave and cabin for all weathers. We will build a home to live in."

Lady Eleanor said:

"My sweet Llewelyn, though this sweet be gall,

"Patience does conquer by out-suffering all."

Llewelyn appeared to be playful, but his wife realized that he must be suffering bitterness — gall — because of the failure of his rebellion. He had hoped to become King of England.

Her advice to him was to be patient and endure his suffering. Patience and endurance would conquer in the end.

Friar Hugh ap David said:

"Now, Mannock-deny, I bet you a penny,

"You shall have neither sheep nor goat

"But Friar David will fleece his coat:

"Wherever Jack, my novice, jet [struts],

"All is fish with him that comes to net;

"David, this year you pay no debt."

Friar Hugh ap David expected that he and Jack the novice would have a good year and a good income. He and Jack would fleece whatever could be fleeced. The sheep, goats, and fishes would include travelers — chances are, some travelers would be unwary.

Everyone except Mortimer exited.

Mortimer said:

"Why, Friar, is it so plain, indeed? Are your intentions so obvious?

"Llewelyn, are you so completely resolved to revel and to roost so near the King?

"What! Shall we have a passage kept in Wales for men-at-arms and adventurous knights?

"By cock, Sir Rice ap Meredith, I see no reason why young Mortimer should not make one among your group and play his part on Mannock-deny here because of his love for his beloved Lady Eleanor."

"By cock" was a euphemism for "by God."

Mortimer continued:

"His Eleanor! If she were Mortimer's, I know, the bitter northern wind upon the plains, the damp vapors that rise from out the marshy grounds, and the influence of contagious, disease-spreading air would not touch her.

"Instead, she should court it — live in a luxurious court — with the proudest dames, wear rich attire, eat sumptuously, and take her ease in beds of softest down.

"Why, Mortimer, may not your offers of love move Lady Eleanor, and win sweet Eleanor away from Llewelyn's love?

"Why, pleasant gold and gentle eloquence have enticed and won over the chastest nymphs, the fairest dames. And vaunts of words and the delights of wealth and ease have caused a nun to yield.

"Llewelyn's Sun is setting and sees the last of desperate chance.

"Why should so fair a star as Lady Eleanor stand in a valley, and not be seen to sparkle in the sky?

"It is enough to cause Jove, King of the gods, to change his glittering robes to see Mnemosyne — and he flies to her."

Jupiter slept with Mnemosyne, the goddess of memory, nine nights in a row; she gave birth to the Nine Muses.

Mortimer then addressed you, the audience:

"Masters, let's go after gentle Robin Hood. You're not so well accompanied, I hope, that you can't accept one more.

"If a potter should come to play his part, you'll give him stripes with a lash or give him welcome, good or worse."

Mortimer was planning to disguise himself as a potter and join Llewelyn's band so he could be close to Lady Eleanor and try to entice her to leave Llewelyn and instead be with him.

He said to himself, "Go, Mortimer, and make love-holidays and court Lady Eleanor.

"The King will accept a common excuse from you for your absence — he has more men than Mortimer to attend on him."

CHAPTER 8

On Mannock-deny in Wales, Llewelyn, Rice ap Meredith, Friar Hugh ap David, the Lady Eleanor, and their train of attendants were gathered. They were all clad in green, and they sang the song "Blithe and Bonny":

A blithe and bonny country lass,
heigh ho, the bonny lass!
Sat sighing on the tender grass
and weeping said, will none come woo her.
A smicker [handsome] boy, a lither swain,
heigh ho, a smicker [handsome] swain!
That in his love was wanton fain [joyous],
with smiling looks straight came unto her.
Whenas the wanton wench espied,
heigh ho, when she espied!
The means to make herself a bride,
she simpered smooth like Bonnybell:
The swain, that saw her squint-eyed kind,
heigh ho, squint-eyed kind!
His arms about her body twined,
and: "Fair lass, how fare ye, well?"
The country kit [kitten (girl, young woman)] said: "Well, forsooth,
heigh ho, well forsooth!
But that I have a longing tooth,
a longing tooth that makes me cry."
"Alas!" said he, "what gars [causes] thy grief?
heigh ho, what gars [causes] thy grief?"
"A wound," quoth she, "without relief,
I fear a maid [maiden, virgin] that I shall die."
"If that be all," the shepherd said,
heigh ho, the shepherd said!
"I'll make thee wive it, gentle maid,
and so recure [heal] thy malady."

Hereon they kissed with many an oath,

heigh ho, with many an oath!

And fore [before] God Pan did plight their troth [pledge their truth (say their marriage vows)],

and to the church they hied [hurried] them fast.

And God send every pretty peat [girl, young woman],

heigh ho, the pretty peat!

That [Who] fears to die of this conceit,

so kind a friend [lover] to help at last.

Once the song had ended, Llewelyn said, "Why, so, I see, my mates, of old, all were not lies that beldames — old women — told about Robin Hood and Little John, Friar Tuck and Maid Marian."

Friar Hugh ap David agreed: "Aye, indeed, master."

Llewelyn continued, "How well they lived in the green forest, frolicsome and lively without trouble, and spent their days in games and glee.

"Llewelyn, seek if anything pleases you, and do not, although your foot be out of town, allow your eyes to look black at and frown angrily at King Edward's crown. And do not think that this green clothing we are wearing is not as gay as was the golden rich array we wore at the court."

He said to Lady Eleanor, "And if, sweet Nell, my Marian, trusts me, as I am a gentleman,

"I say that you are as fine in this attire,

"As fine and fit to my desire,

"As when of Leicester's hall and bower

"You were the rose and sweetest flower."

Lady Eleanor's father was the Earl of Leicester; at his court, she had been richly dressed.

Llewelyn then asked Friar Hugh ap David:

"What do you say, Friar? Do I speak well?

"For anything becomes [looks good on] my Nell."

Friar Hugh ap David replied:

"Never made man of a woman born

"A bullock's tail a blowing horn."

No man can make something into something else it was not born to be. Lady Eleanor was born noble, and no man can change that.

He continued:

"Nor can an ass' hide disguise

"A lion, if he ramp and rise."

Even the wearing of green rustic clothing cannot disguise Lady Eleanor's nobility.

Lady Eleanor said to her husband, "My lord, the Friar is wondrous wise."

Llewelyn, her husband, replied, "Believe him, for he tells no lies."

He then asked Rice ap Meredith, who was taking the part of Little John in this play-acting, and who was silent, "But what is Little John thinking?"

Rice ap Meredith replied, "That Robin Hood should beware of spies.

"An aged saying and a true,

"Black will take no other hue;

"He who of old has been your foe

"Will die but will continue so."

Black cloth cannot be dyed another color, and evil stays evil.

An enemy who has been an enemy for a long time will remain an enemy until — and after — death.

Friar Hugh ap David said:

"Oh, masters, where shall we go?

"Does any living creature know?"

Llewelyn replied:

"Rice ap Meredith and I will walk the round.

"Friar, see about the ground,

"And despoil what prey is to be found."

Llewelyn and Rice ap Meredith would walk in the forest and scout, while the Friar would stay in the camp with Lady Eleanor. Should any edible animal come around, the Friar would try to kill it. Perhaps he could also rob an unwary traveler.

Llewelyn continued:

"My love I leave within your trust,

"Because I know your actions are just."

Actually, Friar Hugh ap David's actions had not always been just. As a Friar, he had sworn to be celibate but had courted a wench.

As Llewelyn and Rice ap Meredith were leaving the camp, Mortimer entered the scene, disguised as a potter.

Llewelyn said, "Come, potter, come, and welcome, too.

"Fare as we fare, and do as we do."

Llewelyn then said to Lady Eleanor, "Nell, adieu. We go for news."

Llewelyn and Rice ap Meredith exited.

The disguised Mortimer stayed a short distance from the camp.

Friar Hugh ap David and Lady Eleanor thought that Mortimer had gone with Llewelyn and Rice ap Meredith, and so they thought they were alone together.

Friar Hugh ap David said to himself:

"A little serves the Friar's lust,

"When *nolens volens* fast I must:

"Master, at all that you refuse."

Nolens is Latin for "unwillingly" or "involuntarily," and *volens* is Latin for "willingly" or "voluntarily." The Friar is supposed to be celibate whether willingly or unwillingly.

The Friar, however, is unwilling to be celibate and therefore he will try to get a little — a kiss, or more — whenever an opportunity — such as now — presented itself.

Gamblers cried "at all" when risking everything on a single throw. The Friar was going to risk everything by attempting to seduce Lady Eleanor while he was alone — he thought — with her.

Llewelyn had "refused" Lady Eleanor by leaving her behind in the camp.

Mortimer, who could hear Friar Hugh ap David clearly, said to himself:

"Such a potter would I choose,

"When I mean to blind an excuse."

A blind excuse is "a poor excuse" or "a sorry shrift." The Friar was a sorry excuse for a Friar when it came to celibacy.

In addition, Mortimer, who was disguised as a potter, was choosing to be and act like the Friar. The Friar is at a sorry shrift because of his vow of celibacy, but he chooses to ignore it and pursue women. Mortimer is at a sorry shrift because he loves a married woman, but he chooses to ignore her marriage vows and pursue that woman. Neither the Friar nor Mortimer can have a good excuse for going against holy vows.

The disguised Mortimer continued:

"While Robin walks with Little John,

"The Friar will lick — kiss — his Marian:
"So will the potter if he can."
Lady Eleanor said:
"Now, Friar, since your lord is gone,
"And you and I are left alone,
"What can the Friar do or say
"To pass the weary time away?
"Weary, God knows, poor wench, to thee,
"Who never thought these days to see."
Llewelyn was trying to enjoy their time in the forest, but Lady Eleanor, although she wanted to be with her husband, preferred life in the court to life in the forest.
The disguised Mortimer said to himself:
"Break, heart! And split, my eyes, in twain!
"Never let me hear those words again."
He hated to hear that Lady Eleanor was unhappy.
(But perhaps he didn't want to suffer much pain on her behalf — his eyes were already split in twain!)
Friar Hugh ap David said:
"What can the Friar do or say
"To pass the weary time away?
"More dare he do than he dare say,
"Because he doubts to get away."
What he wanted to do was seduce Lady Eleanor, but attempting that was risky because of her husband. If he were caught, he might not be able to get away.
Lady Eleanor requested:
"Do something, Friar, speak or sing,
"That may to sorrows solace bring;
"And I meanwhile will garlands make."
The garlands were wreaths made of flowers.
The disguised Mortimer said to himself:
"Oh, Mortimer, were it for your sake,
"A garland were the happiest stake
"That ever this unhappy hand drew!"

If only Lady Eleanor were making the wreath for him, he would value it more that any gambling wager he had ever won.

Friar Hugh ap David said:

"Mistress, shall I tell you true?"

A "mistress" is a female head of household.

The Friar continued:

"I have a song, I learned it long ago:

"I don't know whether you'll like it well or no.

"It is short and sweet, but somewhat brawled before:

"Once let me sing it, and I ask no more."

In this context, "brawled" means "sung clamorously."

Lady Eleanor said:

"What, Friar, will you so indeed?

"Agrees it somewhat with your need?"

Friar Hugh ap David's need — that is, desire — was not to be celibate. The song he had in mind was possibly a bawdy drinking song.

He asked, "Why, mistress, shall I sing my creed?"

He could instead sing a religious song.

Lady Eleanor said, "That's the fitter of the two at need."

Since now was a time of trouble, a religious song was more appropriate.

The disguised Mortimer said to himself: "Oh, wench, how may you hope to speed and succeed?"

The disguised Mortimer knew that Friar Hugh ap David was unlikely to stick to religious songs — or to obey his religious vows.

Friar Hugh ap David said to himself:

"Oh, mistress, out it goes:

"Look what comes next — the Friar throws."

He was about to take his chance at seducing Lady Eleanor.

He sat beside her in preparation to sing — and seduce.

The disguised Mortimer said:

"Such a sitting who ever saw?

"An eagle's bird beside a jackdaw."

Lady Eleanor's was the eagle's fledgling, while the Friar was a much less majestic bird — a small crow.

Lady Eleanor said to the Friar, "So, sir, is this all?"

The disguised Mortimer came forward, revealing himself, and said, "Sweetheart, here's no more."

Lady Eleanor said:

"How are you now, good fellow!

"We are more indeed by one than we were before."

Friar Hugh ap David said, "What now! The devil instead of a ditty!"

The disguised Mortimer replied,

"Friar, a ditty

"Come recently from the city …"

"To ask some pity

"Of this lass so pretty."

He then said to Lady Eleanor, "Give me some pity, sweet mistress, please."

Lady Eleanor asked, "What's going on, Friar? Where are we now, and you play not the man?"

Friar Hugh ap David was supposed to be her protector while her husband and Rice ap Meredith were away. He should be standing up for her and accosting the potter.

Friar Hugh ap David said:

"Friend copesmate, you who

"Came recently from the city,

A "copesmate" is a friend or partner.

The Friar continued:

"To ask some pity

"Of this lass so pretty,

"In likeness of a doleful ditty,

"Hang me if I do not pay ye."

The Friar was saying to hang him if he did not beat the potter.

"Oh, Friar, you grow choleric and angry," the disguised Mortimer said. "Well, you want to have no man court your mistress but yourself. On my word, I'll take you down a button-hole."

Friar Hugh ap David replied, "You talk, you talk, child. You are nothing but talk, boy."

The disguised Mortimer and the Friar began to fight.

As they were fighting, Llewelyn and Rice ap Meredith returned to the camp, and the disguised Mortimer and the Friar stopped fighting.

Llewelyn said, "It is well, potter; you fight in a good quarrel."

The potter had been fighting well. Of course, Mortimer was an experienced military man, although Llewelyn did not recognize him.

Rice ap Meredith took Mortimer's staff, looked it over, and said, "By the Mass, this 'sword' will hold."

He then said, "Let me see your staff, Friar."

Friar Hugh ap David said, "Mine's for my own turn, my own use, I promise you. Give him back his tools."

The Friar then said to the disguised Mortimer, "Rise, and let's go to it — but no change, if you love me. I scorn the odds, I can tell you."

The Friar thought that the disguised Mortimer's staff was longer than the Friar's staff, but the Friar was still willing to fight him. Or, perhaps, he thought that Mortimer was the better fighter.

When two men are dueling, the weapons — whether swords or staffs — ought to be of equal length in order for the fight to be fair.

Friar Hugh ap David then said to Llewelyn and Rice ap Meredith, "See fair play, if you are gentlemen."

Llewelyn and Rice ap Meredith would be the referees of the fight.

Llewelyn replied, "By the Virgin Mary, we shall be, Friar."

Llewelyn checked the two staffs, saying, "Let us see. Are their staffs of a similar length? Good.

"So, now let us decide the matter,

"Friar and potter, without more clatter.

"I have cast your water,

"And see as deep into your desire,

"As any man who had dived every day into your bosom."

In this society, doctors cast water — that is, they examined the patient's urine and diagnosed illnesses when they were present.

The illness of both the Friar and the potter was lust. Llewelyn could guess that they were fighting over Lady Eleanor.

Llewelyn then said to Friar Hugh ap David:

"Oh, Friar, will nothing serve your turn but larks?

"Are such fine birds for such coarse clerks?

"None but my Marian can serve your turn?"

"Clerks" (pronounced "clarks") are clerics.

Lady Eleanor said, "Cast water, for the house will burn."

She was capable of wit and punning.

Friar Hugh ap David said:

"Oh, mistress, mistress, flesh is frail;

"Beware when the sign is in the tail:

"Mighty is love and it does prevail."

"Beware when the sign is in the tail" is good advice for Friar Hugh ap David. A wedding ring on a woman's finger is a sign or symbol that this tail is taken. The sign can literally be in the tail when fingering occurs.

Llewelyn said:

"Therefore, Friar, shall you not fail,

"But mightily your foe assail,

"And thrash this potter with your flail."

A flail is used in threshing grain. It has a short free-swinging club attached to a longer wooden handle. Llewelyn was punning: "to thrash" meant "to beat up" and "to thresh."

Llewelyn then said:

"And, potter, never rave nor rail,

"Nor ask questions what I ail [about what ails me],

"But take this tool, and do not quail,

"But thrash this Friar's russet coat;

"And make him sing a dastard's note."

A "dastard" is a coward.

He continued:

"And cry, *Peccavi miserere David*

"*In amo amavi*.

"Go to it."

The Latin means, "I have sinned. Have pity on David [that is, the Friar] in that I have loved."

The disguised Mortimer said, "Strike! Strike!"

Friar Hugh ap David said:

"Strike, potter, be thou lief or loath [willing or unwilling]:

"If you'll not strike, I'll strike for both."

The disguised Mortimer struck the Friar and then said:

"He must needs [necessarily] go whom the devil drives.

"So, then, Friar, beware of other men's wives."

Friar Hugh ap David said:

"I wish, master arrogant potter, that the devil will have my soul.

"As long as I'll make my flail circumscribe your noll."

"Circumscribe your noll" meant "make a circle on your head." Of course, the Friar's tonsure made a circle on his head.

The Friar struck the disguised Mortimer.

Llewelyn said:

"Why, so; now it cottons [goes well]. Now the game begins.

"One knave curries [beats] another for his sins."

Friar Hugh ap David knelt before Llewelyn and said, "Oh, master, shorten my offences in your eyes! Forgive me for my offense!"

He added:

"If this crucifix I am wearing does not suffice,

"Send me to Heaven in a hempen sacrifice."

Friar Hugh ap David wanted Llewelyn to forgive him. If Llewelyn would not forgive him, the Friar wanted to be hung with a hempen rope and then go to Heaven.

The disguised Mortimer knelt before Llewelyn and Rice ap Meredith and said:

"Oh, masters, masters, let this be warning!

"The Friar has infected me with his learning."

Llewelyn said:

"Villains, do not touch the forbidden tree,

"Now to delude or to dishonor me."

In other words, leave Lady Eleanor (the forbidden tree) alone.

Friar Hugh ap David said, "Oh, master, *quae negata sunt grata sunt.*"

The Latin means, "Things that are denied are pleasing."

Llewelyn said to Rice ap Meredith:

"Rice, every day thus shall it be:

"We'll have a thrashing set among the Friars; and he

"Who of these challengers lays on the slowest load,

"Be thou at hand, Rice ap Meredith, to gore him with your goad."

Llewelyn used the word "Friars" because the potter had admitted that the Friar had "infected" him with the Friar's "learning."

Llewelyn wanted the Friar and the potter to fight each day. Rice ap Meredith would use a goad to force the person who held back the most at fighting to fight harder.

Friar Hugh ap David said:

"Ah, potter, potter, the Friar may rue

"That ever this day this our quarrel he knew;

"My pate [head] is addled [foggy (from being beaten)]; my arms are black and blue."

The disguised Mortimer replied:

"Ah, Friar, who may his fate's force eschew?

"I think, Friar, you are prettily schooled."

In other words, no one can escape his fate, and you, the Friar, have learned a lesson.

Friar Hugh ap David replied, "And I think the potter is handsomely cooled."

In other words, you, the potter, have received your share of blows that cooled your ardor.

Everyone exited the scene except the disguised Mortimer, who said to himself:

"No, Mortimer; here's that eternal fire

"That burns and flames with firebrands of hot desire.

"Why, Mortimer, why don't you discover [reveal]

"Yourself [to be] her knight, her liegeman [faithful follower], and her lover?"

CHAPTER 9

At Berwick, on the border of Scotland and England, were John Baliol, who was now King of Scots, and his train of attendants, who included Lord Versses and some French Lords.

King Baliol of Scotland said, "Lords of Albania, and my peers in France, since Baliol is invested in his rights as King of Scotland, and wears the royal Scottish diadem, it is time to rouse him so that the world may know that Scotland disdains to carry England's yoke."

Albania was an ancient name for Scotland.

King Baliol continued, "Therefore, my friends, thus prepared in readiness for war, why do we waste time and delay greeting the English King with a resolute message that will let him know our minds and our demands?

"Lord Versses, although your faith and oath have been taken to follow Baliol's arms for Scotland's right, yet your heart is knit to England's honor. Although you have pledged to follow me, I know that you are still partial to England.

"Therefore, to spite England and yourself, you will bear defiance proudly to your King: Edward I. Tell him that Albania finds heart and hope to shake off England's tyranny at once and to rescue Scotland's honor with the sword.

"Lord Bruce, see cast about Versses' neck a strangling halter, so that he remembers to do this task in haste."

Lord Robert Bruce was the grandfather of the great King Robert the Bruce of Scotland. Robert the Bruce was born on 11 July 1274.

King Baliol was demeaning Versses by requiring him to wear a noose around his neck as he performed the task of delivering Baliol's defiant message to King Edward I. The noose was a reminder of what would happen to him if he did not perform his task well and quickly.

Not using the respectful "you," King Baliol asked, "What do thou, Versses? Will thou deliver this message?"

Versses replied, "Although no common post, yet, for my King, I will go to England, despite England's might, and do my errand boldly, as is fitting although I honor English Edward's name and hold this slavish contemptible noose in scorn."

Using the royal "we," King Baliol said, "Then hurry away, as swift as a swallow flies, and meet me on our inroads into England's ground. While we are there, we will think of your message and your haste."

In other words, perform this task well and quickly, or the noose will strangle you.

CHAPTER 10

— SCENE X —

At Carnarvon Castle in Wales, King Edward I, Edmund Duke of Lancaster (the King's brother), Gloucester, Sussex, Sir David, and Cressingham (a noble) arrived. They were still wearing their riding boots after travelling on horseback from Northampton, which was located 60 miles north-west of London. They stood outside the Queen's tent. Queen Eleanor had recently delivered a son in Wales, as King Edward had wanted.

King Edward I said, "Now I have time, lords, to give you welcome to Wales.

"Welcome, sweet Edmund, to christen your young nephew.

"And welcome, Cressingham; give me your hand.

"But, Sussex, what has become of Mortimer? We have not seen the man for many days."

The Earl of Sussex replied, "Before your highness rode from here to Northampton, Sir Roger Mortimer was a suitor to your grace concerning fair Lady Eleanor, Llewelyn's love. He wanted to marry her, but she was given to Llewelyn in exchange for Sir David.

"And since his suit was denied, it seems likely that he, discontented, stays away from your royal presence."

King Edward I said, "Why, Sussex, didn't we say to Lady Eleanor that as long as she would leave Llewelyn, whom she had loved too long, she might have favor with my Queen and me?

"But, man, her mind above her fortune mounts,

"And that's a cause she fails in her accounts."

In other words, in his opinion Lady Eleanor had made the wrong decision: She would stay with Llewelyn, although her way of life would have been much richer and more luxurious if she had stayed with King Edward I and had rejected Llewelyn.

King Edward I continued, "But go with me, my Lord Edmund of Lancaster. We will go see my beauteous lovely Queen, who has enriched me with a splendid boy."

The Queen's tent opened, revealing Queen Eleanor sitting up in her bed, attended by the Duchess of Lancaster, Joan of Acre, Mary (the Mayoress of

London), and other attendants. The Queen was dandling her young son on her knee.

King Edward, Edmund, and Gloucester went into the Queen's chamber.

King Edward I said, "Ladies, by your leave."

He was politely requesting the permission of the Queen's attendants to visit the Queen. Such permission, of course, was readily granted.

He asked:

"How is my Nell, my own, my love, my life,

"My heart, my dear, my dove, my Queen, my wife?"

Queen Eleanor replied, "Ned, have you come, sweet Ned? Welcome, my joy! Your Nell presents you with a lovely boy. Kiss him, and christen him after your own name."

Edward's son would be named Edward.

She continued, "Heigh-ho! Whom do I see? My Lord Edmund of Lancaster! Welcome heartily."

"Heigh-ho" indicated fatigue.

Edmund Duke of Lancaster replied, "I thank your grace. Sweet Nell, we are well met. This is a good meeting."

Referring to her baby boy, Queen Eleanor said, "Brother Edmund, here's a kinsman of yours. You must be acquainted with him."

Edmund Duke of Lancaster was the boy's uncle and Queen Eleanor's brother-in-law.

Edmund Duke of Lancaster replied, "A splendid boy. God bless him!"

He said to the baby boy, "Give me your hand, sir. You are welcome into Wales."

He put his finger on one of the boy's palms, and the boy's fingers curled around it.

Queen Eleanor said, "Brother, there's a fist, I promise you, that will hold a mace as tightly as ever did his father or grandfather before him."

The boy's father and grandfather, of course, were King Edward I and Edward I's father, King Henry III.

King Edward I said:

"But tell me now, wrapped in lily bands [white cloth],

"How with my Queen and my lovely boy it stands,

"After your journey and these childbed pains?"

He was asking how his wife and son were. Queen Eleanor had undergone a rigorous journey and had recently given birth.

Queen Eleanor replied:

"Sick, my own Ned, is your Nell for your company;

"You who lured her with your lies all so far,

"To follow you unwieldy [awkwardly] in your war."

Queen Eleanor had to be told by Gloucester why her husband had required her to come to Wales: He wanted their son to be born in Wales and thereby become eligible to be Prince of Wales and rule Wales.

She continued:

"But I forgive you, Ned, my life's delight.

"So long as you see that your young son will be bravely dight [finely dressed],

"And in Carnarvon christened royally.

"Sweet love, let him be lapped [wrapped] most curiously [handsomely]:

"He is thine own, as true as he is mine;

"Take order, then, that he be passing fine."

"Passing fine" meant "surpassingly finely dressed."

King Edward I replied:

"My lovely lady, let that care be your least:

"For my young son the country will I feast,

"And have him borne [carried] as bravely [splendidly dressed] to the font [baptismal fountain]

"As ever yet King's son to christening went.

"Lack thou no precious thing to comfort thee,

"[Thou who are d]earer than England's diadem to me."

Queen Eleanor replied, "Thanks, gentle lord."

She then said:

"Nurse, rock the cradle: fie [bah, or darn it],

"The King so near, and he hear the boy cry.

"Joan, take him up, and sing a lullaby."

Joan, her daughter, picked up the boy and soothed him.

King Edward I said, "It is well, believe me, girl. Thank you, Joan!"

Edmund Duke of Lancaster said, "She learns, my lord, to lull a young one of her own."

Queen Eleanor requested, "Give me something to drink."

King Edward I replied:

"Drink nectar, my sweet Nell,

"You who are worthy for a seat in Heaven with Jove to dwell."

Nectar is the drink of the gods, and Jove, aka Jupiter, is the King of the gods.

Queen Eleanor drank and said, "Thank you, Ned. Now, I remember; I have a suit — a request — to ask of you, sweet lord, and you must not deny it."

"Where's my Lord of Gloucester, good Clare [Gloucester's family name], my host, my guide?"

Gloucester had guided her during the trip to Wales.

"Good Ned, let Joan of Acre be his bride.

"Assure yourself that they are thoroughly wooed."

She was reassuring the King that this was not a sudden passion; Gloucester had been wooing Joan for a long time.

Gloucester said to himself, "May God send the King an agreeable mood!"

Edmund Duke of Lancaster said, "Then, niece, it is likely that you shall have a husband."

King Edward I said, "Come here, Gloucester. Now, give her your hand. Take her, sole daughter to the Queen of England."

Joan and Gloucester held hands.

King Edward I said:

"For the news he brought, Nell, of my young son,

"I promised him as much as I have done."

It was Gloucester who had ridden to Northampton to give him the good news that he was the father of a son in Wales. Edward had promised to reward the messenger who brought him good news, and he was now fulfilling his promise.

Still holding hands, Gloucester and Joan said, "We humbly thank your majesty."

Edmund Duke of Lancaster said, "May much joy fall to them. A gallant bridegroom and a princely bride!"

King Edward I said, "Now say, sweet Queen, what does my lady crave? Tell me what name this young Welshman shall have, who was born Prince of Wales by Cambria's full consent?"

Of course, *Cambria* is another name for *Wales*. The Welsh name for the country is *Cymru*, and *Cambria* is its Latinized form.

Queen Eleanor replied, "Edward is the name that makes me well content."

"Then Edward of Carnarvon shall he be," King Edward I said, "and Prince of Wales, christened in royalty."

Seeing that Queen Eleanor looked tired, Edmund Duke of Lancaster said, "My lord, I think the Queen would like to take a nap."

Joan said, "Nurse, take the child, and hold him in your lap."

King Edward I said, "Farewell, good Joan. Take care of my Queen.

"Sleep, Nell, the fairest swan my eyes have seen."

They closed the tent opening, and Sussex exited.

Edmund Duke of Lancaster said to the King, "I forgot to ask your majesty what do you intend to do about the rebels here in Wales?"

King Edward I said, "I intend to do what Kings do with rebels, Mun; our right prevails."

"Mun" was his nickname for Edmund Duke of Lancaster.

King Edward I continued, "We have good Robin Hood and Little John, the Friar and the good Maid Marian. Why, our Llewelyn is a mighty man."

He was aware that the Welsh rebels were living in the mountains.

"Trust me, my lord," Gloucester said, "I think it would be very good if some good fellows went and scoured the wood, and made it their task to beat Robin Hood. I think the Friar, for all his lusty looks, and Robin's rabble with their glaives and hooks would be quickly driven to the nooks."

"Glaives and hooks" are pole-weapons. At the end of a glaive is a blade. At the end of a Welsh hook is a curved blade and a spike.

Sir David said, "I can assure your highness of what I know: The false, traitorous Llewelyn will not run nor go, nor will that proud rebel called Little John, nor will they give an inch of ground, come man for man, to him who wields the weightiest sword of England."

He was saying that the Welsh would fight ferociously, something that Gloucester disagreed with.

Gloucester said, "Welshman, how will you speak so that we understand?"

The words he would understand were words that praised the English side and dispraised the rebels.

He continued:

"But what you say about Llewelyn, David, I deny.

"England has men who will make Llewelyn fly [flee],

"Maugre [Despite] his beard, and hide him in a hole,

"Weary of England's dints and manly dole."

"Maugre his beard" means "despite his manliness" or "despite what he can do."

"Dints" are blows and "dole" is the giving of something — in this case, it is the giving of blows.

Edmund Duke of Lancaster said, "Gloucester, don't be so angry that you make every argument a defense of England's honor."

King Edward I said, "By Gis, fair lords, before many days have passed, England shall give this Robin Hood his breakfast."

"By Gis" is an oath using a euphemistic pronunciation of "Jesus."

Llewelyn's "breakfast" would be defeat.

King Edward I then said, "Sir David, friend, keep what I say secret if I use your skill. You know the way to where this proud Robin and his yeomen roam."

He wanted to ambush Llewelyn and the other rebels in their mountain camp. He trusted Sir David enough to tell him secrets and to use Sir David's knowledge.

"I do, my lord," Sir David said, "and I can run blindfold there."

"Sir David, enough," King Edward I said. "As I am a gentleman, I'll have one merry flirt with Little John, and Robin Hood, and his Maid Marian.

"Be thou my counsel and my company,

"And thou may the King of England's resolution see."

The Earl of Sussex returned and said, "May it please your majesty, here are four good squires of the cantreds where they do dwell, come in the name of the whole country to congratulate your highness on all your good fortunes, and by me offer their most humble service to your young son, their Prince, whom they most heartily beseech God to bless with long life and honor."

A squire's rank is just below that of a knight.

These Welsh squires were also called barons.

Cantreds are geographical units consisting of a hundred townships.

King Edward I replied, "Well said, Sussex. Please tell them to come near."

Sussex exited.

King Edward I said, "Sir David, trust me, this is kindly done by your countrymen."

Sir David said to himself, "They are villains, traitors to the ancient glory and renown of Cambria!"

Sussex returned with the four barons of Wales. He carried a blanket made of coarse wool. The barons knelt.

Recognizing two of them, Sir David said to himself, "Morris Vaughan, are you there? And you, proud Lord of Anglesey?"

The first Welsh baron said, "The poor country of Cambria, by us unworthy messengers, congratulates your majesty on the birth of your young son, Prince of Wales, and in this poor gift express their most zealous duty and affection, which with all humbleness we present to your highness' sweet and sacred hands."

The gift was the blanket.

King Edward I said, "Thank you, barons, for your gifts and good-wills. By this means my boy shall wear a mantle of the Welsh people's weaving to keep him warm, and so my boy shall live for England's honor and Cambria's good. I shall not need, I trust, courteously to invite you to the christening."

He meant that they should already know that they were welcome.

He continued, "I don't doubt, lords, that you will be all in readiness to wait on your young Prince, and do him honor at his christening."

The Earl of Sussex said, "The whole country of Cambria round about, all well-horsed and attended on, both men and women in their best array, have come down to do service of love and honor to our recently born Prince, your majesty's son and heir.

"The men and women of Snowdon especially have sent in a great abundance of cattle and corn, enough by computation to feed your highness' household a whole month and more."

King Edward I said, "We thank them all, and we will present our Queen with these courtesies and presents bestowed on her young son, and greatly account you as our friends."

The four Welsh barons exited.

The Queen's tent opened, and the King, his brother Edmund Duke of Lancaster, and the Earl of Gloucester entered.

Queen Eleanor asked, "Who is talking there?"

"A friend, madam," King Edward I answered.

Joan said, "Madam, it is the King."

"Welcome, my lord," Queen Eleanor said. "Heigh-ho, what have we there?"

She was looking at the woolen blanket.

Using the royal plural, King Edward I said, "Madam, the Welsh people, in all kindness and duty, recommend their service and good-will to your son, and in token of their pure good-will present to him by us a blanket made of frieze, richly lined to keep him warm."

Frieze is coarse wool cloth.

Queen Eleanor said, "A blanket made of frieze! Bah! Bah! For God's sake, let me hear no more of it, if you love me. Bah, my lord! Is this the wisdom and kindness of the Welsh people?

"Now I commend me to them all, and if Wales have no more wit or manners than to clothe a King's son in frieze, I have a blanket in store for my boy that shall, I think, make him shine like the Sun, and perfume the streets where he comes."

She wanted their son to be clothed in expensive fabric, but wool is a warm fabric and in cold weather warm fabric is better than not-warm expensive fabric.

King Edward I said, "In good time, madam — he is your own, so wrap him as you wish, but I promise you, Nell, I would not for ten thousand pounds want the Welsh people to take unkindness at your words."

The Welsh people would be insulted by Queen Eleanor's rejection of their gift to her son.

Queen Eleanor replied, "It is no wonder, I am sure: You have been royally received at their hands.

"No, Ned, your Nell can't do as she wishes. If she could, her boy would glisten like the summer's Sun in robes as rich as those of Jove when he triumphs. His baby food would be made of precious nectar, and his food would be ambrosia — no earthly woman's milk for him.

"Sweet fires of cinnamon would warm him. The goddesses known as the three Graces would attend on his cradle, Venus would make his bed and wait on him, and Phoebus' daughter would always sing him asleep."

Phoebus Apollo's only daughter was Parthenos, who became the constellation Virgo after an early death. Her mother was Chrysothemis. "Parthenos" means "the virgin."

Queen Eleanor continued:

"Thus would I have my boy treated as divine,

"Because he is King Edward's son and mine:

"And do you mean to wrap him up in a blanket made of frieze?

"For God's sake store it away charily — carefully — and perfume it in readiness for winter; it will make him a goodly warm Christmas coat."

Her instructions to perfume the frieze blanket may mean that to her it stank.

King Edward I said to Edmund Duke of Lancaster, "Ah, Mun, my brother, dearer than my life, how this proud, arrogant temperament slays my heart with grief!"

He wanted his son to rule Wales. A Queen who infuriated the Welsh people could make that unlikely to happen.

He continued, "Sweet Queen, how much I pity the effects — the consequences that can follow your words! This Spanish pride agrees not with England's King, who dislikes it.

"Mild is the mind where honor builds his bower,

"And yet is earthly honor but a flower."

Earthly honor doesn't last long.

He continued, "Fast to those looks are all my fancies tied,

"Pleased with your sweetness, angry with your pride."

Much of his pleasure and displeasure in life came from his Queen. When she was sweet, he felt pleasure. When she was proud and arrogant, as now, he felt anger.

Queen Eleanor said, "Bah! Bah!

"I think that I am not where I should be,

"Or at the least I am not where I would be."

She would prefer not to be in Wales.

King Edward I asked, "What does my Queen lack that would make perfect her contentment? Only ask for it and you will have it. The King will not repent his words: You will get what you ask for."

Queen Eleanor said, "Thanks, gentle Edward.

"Lords, have at you, then!

"Have at you all, long-bearded Englishmen!

"Have at you, lords and ladies, when I crave

"To give your English pride a Spanish brave."

"Have at you!" were words spoken at the beginning of a fight.

A "brave" is an act of defiance or an insult.

King Edward I asked, "What does my Queen mean?"

Gloucester thought to himself, *This is a Spanish fit.*

Queen Eleanor said, "Ned, you have granted this to me, and you cannot revoke it."

King Edward I replied, "Sweet Queen, speak on. My word shall be my deed."

Queen Eleanor said, "Then shall my words make many a bosom bleed.

"Read, Ned, your Queen's request enclosed up in rhyme,

"And say your Nell had skill to choose her time."

She had chosen her time well — a time when her husband must grant to her what she wanted or go back on his word to her. That she had written the note ahead of time indicated that she had prepared for when that time would come.

Queen Eleanor gave King Edward I a piece of paper.

King Edward I read out loud:

"*The pride of Englishmen's long hair*

"*Is more than England's Queen can bear:*

"*Women's right breasts, cut them off all;*

"*And let the great tree perish with the small.*"

The last line may mean: Let the great and not-great people of England be humiliated.

King Edward I then asked her, "What means my lovely Eleanor by this?"

Queen Eleanor replied, "I mean not to be denied, for it is my request."

Edmund Duke of Lancaster said, "Gloucester, this is an often-said old saying:

"He who grants all that is asked,

"Is much harder than Hercules tasked."

Gloucester said to himself:

"If the King were as mad as the Queen is wood,

82

"Here would be an end of England's good."

The words "mad" and "wood" both meant "insane."

King Edward I said:

"I gave her my word — I am well agreed.

"Let men's beards molt and women's bosoms bleed!

"Call forth my barbers! Lords, we'll first begin."

He used the royal we to say that he would be the first to have his beard shaved off.

Two barbers entered and King Edward I said:

"Come, sirrah, cut me close to the chin,

"And round me even, see that thou do, by a dish.

"Leave not a lock: my Queen shall have her wish."

This sounds as if the King would also get a bowl haircut in addition to having his beard cut off.

Queen Eleanor said:

"What, Ned, those locks that always pleased your Nell,

"Where her desire, where her delight does dwell!

"Will you deface that silver labyrinth,

"More brilliant than purpled hyacinth?

"Sweet Ned, your sacred person ought not droop,

"Though my command makes other gallants stoop."

In other words, her orders did not apply to him. She was willing to humiliate noblemen, but she would allow her husband to keep his beard and long hair because she liked it. Of course, she was not willing to cut off her own right breast, although she was willing to make English ladies do that.

King Edward I replied:

"Madam, pardon me and pardon all.

"No justice but the great runs with the small."

For justice to be justice, rules must apply to the great (the upper class) as well as to the small (the other classes).

He then asked, "Tell me, good Gloucester, aren't you afeard [afraid]?"

"No, my lord," Gloucester replied, "but I am resolved to lose my beard."

King Edward I said to Queen Eleanor:

"Now, madam, if you purpose to proceed

"To make so many guiltless ladies bleed,

"Here must the law begin, sweet Eleanor, at your breast,

"And stretch itself with violence to the rest.

"Else kings ought no other do,

"Fair lady, than they would be done unto."

This is the Golden Rule: "Treat others as you want to be treated. Do not treat others as you do not want to be treated."

Queen Eleanor replied, "What logic do you call this? Is Edward mocking his love?"

She did not want her right breast cut off, and she saw nothing wrong with a rule not applying to a Queen although other women had to follow it.

King Edward I said:

"No, Nell; he does as best in honor does behoove."

In other words, he was behaving as honor demanded.

He continued:

"And he prays to you, gentle Queen — and let my prayers move you to [that is, persuade you to]

"Leave these ungentle thoughts, put on a milder mind;

"Have sweet looks, not lofty — a civil mood becomes a woman's kind:

"And live, as, being dead and buried in the ground,

"You may for affability and honor be renowned."

Queen Eleanor said:

"Nay, if you preach, I pray, my lord, be gone:

"The child will cry and trouble you anon [soon].

The Nurse closed the tent.

The Mayoress and the ladies remained outside the tent.

The Mayoress said to herself:

"*Quo semel est imbuta recens servabit odorem testa diu.*"

The Latin means, "A jar will long retain the odor of what it was dipped in when new."

Mayoress Mary was quoting Horace's *Epistles* (Book 1, Epistle 2, lines 69-70).

She continued speaking to herself:

"Proud incest in the cradle of disdain,"

No biological incest occurred with Queen Eleanor's parents, so the Mayoress may have regarded her as the offspring of disdain and pride.

She continued:

"Bred up in court of pride, brought up in Spain,

"Do you command him coyly from your sight,

"Him who is your star, the glory of your light?"

In this culture, a good wife was a wife who obeyed her husband and who did not cause him unnecessary trouble. But since Queen Eleanor had been badly raised in Spain, according to the Mayoress, Queen Eleanor did not do that.

King Edward I said, "Oh, if only I could with the riches of my crown buy better thoughts for my renowned Nell, your mind, sweet Queen, should be as beautiful as your face, as beautiful as all your features, laden with pure honor's treasure, and enriched with incomparable virtues and glory."

He then ordered, "Ladies, look after her majesty. See that the Queen your mistress does not learn what I now tell you.

"At any hand our pleasure is that our young son be borne in this Welsh blanket to his christening because I have special reasons for this. But when he has left the church, he shall be dressed as best it pleases your women's wits to devise."

The Mayoress and the ladies went into the tent, but Joan stayed outside.

King Edward I then said, "Yet, sweet Joan, see this faithfully performed — and, listen, daughter, look you be not last up when this day comes, lest Gloucester find another bride in your stead."

This was gentle joking. The early bird gets the worm, and a woman up earlier than Joan could get Gloucester.

King Edward I said, "David, come with me."

King Edward and Sir David exited.

Gloucester joked, "She rises early, Joan, whatever woman beguiles you of a Gloucester."

Edmund Duke of Lancaster said to Joan, "Don't believe him, sweet niece. Women can speak smoothly to get an advantage."

In other words, women can be persuasive when it benefits them. This was more gentle joking: He meant that a woman could steal Gloucester from her through flattering him — without the woman rising early.

Joan joked back, "Do you mean 'we MEN' do that, my good uncle? Well, be the accent where it will, women are women."

Accent the second syllable of the word "women" and MEN is stressed.

Joan continued, "I will believe you for as great a matter as this comes to, my lord."

In other words, she would act in such a way that she would not lose Gloucester.

Gloucester said, "Thank you, sweet lady, *et habebis fidei mercedem contra.*"

The Latin means, "And you will be rewarded for your faith."

CHAPTER 11

At Carnorvan Castle in Wales, Jack the novice and his company of musicians arrived to perform music for the Queen at her tent.

Jack the novice said, "Come, fellows, cast yourselves even round in a string — a *ring*, I meant to say. Come merrily on my word, for the Queen is most liberal and generous, and if you will please her well, she will pay you royally. So, la full well to show off your British vigorously to solace our good Queen."

In English, very many non-verb words can be verbed. "La" is a musical syllable, but Jack used it as a verb meaning "sing."

Jack the novice continued, "God save her grace, and give our young Prince a carol in their kind!

"Come on, come on, tune your fiddles, and beat your heads together, and behave handsomely."

Hmm. I think I would prefer to beat my hands together.

They played and sang and then exited.

CHAPTER 12

— SCENE XII —

Near the rebel camp on Mannock-deny, Wales, Friar Hugh ap David thought about cheating a farmer out of his money.

He said, "I smell a wallet with my nose this gay morning, and now will I test how clerkly — cleverly — the Friar, by which I mean me, can behave himself.

"It is a common fashion to get gold by saying, 'Stand, and deliver your purses!' Friar Davy, however, will once in his days get money by the use of his wit and intelligence.

"There is a rich farmer who should pass this way to receive a round sum of money. If he shall come to me, the money is mine, and the law shall take no advantage of me. I will cut off the law as the hangman would cut a man down when he has shaken his heels half-an-hour under the gallows. Well, I must take some pains for this gold, and let's get to it!"

Friar Hugh ap David spread part of his gown on the ground, and then he began to throw dice.

The farmer entered the scene and said, "It is an often-said old saying. I remember I read it in Cato's *Pueriles* that *Cantabit vacuus coram latrone viator*; that is, a man purse-penniless may sing before a thief."

In other words, a man who is penniless is free to go among thieves.

Actually, Leonhard Culmann collected the *Sententiae Pueriles*. The quote, which comes from Juvenal's Satire X, appears in William Lily's *Short Introduction to Grammar*.

The farmer continued, "True, as I have not one penny, which makes me so pertly — briskly and brazenly — pass through these thickets. But indeed I am to receive a hundred marks; and all my concern is how I shall pass this way again. Well, I am resolved either to ride twenty miles round about, or else to be so well accompanied that I will not worry about the rogues who live in this area."

Friar Hugh ap David pretended to be talking to himself, but he spoke loudly enough for the farmer to hear him: "Did ever any man play with such uncircumcised — that is, heathen — hands? Size-ace to eleven and lose the chance!"

He was pretending to be playing at dice and losing. "Size-ace" is a six and a one on a throw of the dice.

The farmer said, "God speed, good fellow! May God send you success! But why are you so very angry? There's nobody who will win your money from you."

Since the Friar was playing dice with himself, he would not lose money. It would simply pass from one of his hands to the other.

Friar Hugh ap David replied, "By God's wounds, you do me injury, sir, when you speak when I cast the dice."

Surprised, the farmer said to himself, "The Friar undoubtedly is a lunatic."

He then said, "I ask you, good fellow, to stop raging and to get some warm drink to comfort your brains."

Friar Hugh ap David said, "Alas, sir, I am not a lunatic. It is not so well, for I have lost my money, which is far worse. I have lost five gold nobles to Saint Francis; and if I knew where to meet with his receiver, I would pay him immediately."

A receiver collects money for another person.

The farmer asked, "Do you want to speak with Saint Francis' receiver?"

"Oh, Lord, yes, sir, very gladly," Friar Hugh ap David said.

The farmer said, "Why, man, I am Saint Francis' receiver, if you have any business to do with him."

Friar Hugh ap David asked, "Are you Saint Francis' receiver? Jesus, Jesus! Are you Saint Francis' receiver? And how is he doing?"

"I am his receiver, and I am now going to him," the farmer said. "He invited Saint Thomas a' Waterings to a calf's-head and bacon breakfast this morning."

St. Francis had died on 3 October 1226. King Edward I had been born in June 1239.

Saint Thomas a' Waterings is a place, but the farmer was using it as if it were the name of a person to mock Friar Hugh ap David and to test if he were really insane.

"Good Lord, sir," Friar Hugh ap David said, "I beg you to carry to him these five nobles, and tell him I deal as honestly with him as if he were here present."

Friar Hugh ap David gave the farmer five nobles.

The farmer replied, "I will do so on my word and honesty, Friar; and so farewell."

"Farewell, Saint Francis' receiver, even heartily," Friar Hugh ap David said.

The farmer exited.

Friar Hugh ap David said, "Well, now the Friar is out of cash five nobles. God knows how he shall come into cash again, but I must go to playing with dice again."

He threw the dice and said, "There's nine for your holiness and six for me."

He was still pretending to play dice with "your holiness" — St. Francis.

Llewelyn, Rice ap Meredith, and Mortimer (still disguised as a potter) entered the scene with some prisoners. They were surviving by hunting and fishing — and by robbing travelers.

"Come on, my hearts," Llewelyn said. "Bring forth your prisoners, and let us see what supply of fish there is in their purse-nets."

The fish were coins.

Seeing and hearing Friar Hugh ap David, Llewelyn said, "Friar, why are you raging, man? Here's nobody who will offer you any foul play, I promise you."

Friar Hugh ap David said, "Oh, good master, give me permission to keep on playing. I have been losing money, but I trust I shall recover my losses."

"The Friar is mad," Llewelyn said, "but let him alone with his device."

A device in this context is a plan or plot; Llewelyn guessed that there was a method to the Friar's "madness."

He then said, "And now to you, my masters, peddler, priest, and piper. Throw down your wallets in the meanwhile, and when the Friar is at leisure he shall tell you what you must do."

The peddler said, "Alas, Sir, I have but three pence in the corner of my shoe."

Rice ap Meredith said, "Never a shoulder of mutton, Piper, in your tabor?"

A tabor is a small drum.

Rice ap Meredith may have meant, "Playing music doesn't pay well, Piper?"

He then said, "But wait! Here comes company."

King Edward Longshanks, Sir David, and the farmer entered the scene. King Edward Longshanks and Sir David were disguised as common travelers.

The farmer said, "Alas, gentlemen, if you love yourselves and want to avoid being robbed, do not venture through this mountain passage: Here's such an uproar with Robin Hood and his rabble that every cross in my purse trembles for fear."

The coins in his wallet, aka purse, had a cross on one side.

The disguised King Edward I replied, "Honest man, as I said to you before, conduct us through this wood, and if you are robbed or have any violence directed at you, as I am a gentleman, I will repay you again."

The disguised Sir David asked, "How much money do you have on you?"

"Truly, sir, a hundred marks," the farmer said. "I received it even now at Brecknock. But, oh, no! We are done for! Yonder is Robin Hood and all the strong thieves in the mountain. I have no hope left but your honor's assurance that you will repay me for my loss."

The disguised King Edward I said, "Don't worry. I will be my word's master: I will do what I said I would do."

Friar Hugh ap David said, "Good master, if you love the Friar, help him for a while, I ask of you, and as you like what I am doing, so love him — me — who holds the dice."

The Friar was asking his master — if the Friar were a Franciscan, that would be St. Francis — for help in cheating the rich farmer. Or he was slyly asking Llewelyn (or the disguised King) for help in cheating the rich farmer. Or both. Or all three.

The farmer asked, "What! Friar, are you still laboring at dice so hard? Will you have anything more to give to Saint Francis?"

"Good Lord, are you here, sweet Saint Francis' receiver?" Friar Hugh ap David said. "How is his holiness doing, and all his good family?"

As a celibate priest, and saint, St. Francis had no biological children.

"He is in good health, truly, Friar," the farmer replied. "Do you have any nobles for him?"

Friar Hugh ap David answered, "You know the dice are not biased. If Saint Francis were ten saints, they will favor him no more than they would favor the devil, if he should play at dice. In very truth, my friend, they have favored the Friar, and I have won a hundred marks from Saint Francis. Come, sir; please, sirrah, hand it over: I know, sirrah, he is a good man, and never deceives none."

"Hand it over!" the farmer said. "What do you mean by that?"

Friar Hugh ap David answered, "Why, *in numeratis pecuniis legem pone.*"

He then loosely translated the Latin: "Pay me my winnings."

"What an ass is this Friar!" the farmer said. "Why should I pay you your winnings?"

Friar Hugh ap David asked, "Why, aren't you, sirrah, Saint Francis' receiver?"

"Indeed, I do receive money for Saint Francis," the farmer replied.

"Then I'll make you pay for Saint Francis, that's certain," Friar Hugh ap David said.

The two men fought.

The farmer shouted, "Help, help! I am robbed, I am robbed!"

The disguised King Edward I said, "Villain, you wrong the man. Hands off!"

Friar Hugh ap David said, "Masters, I beg you to stop this brawling and give me permission to speak. This is how it is. I went to dice with Saint Francis, and lost five nobles. By good fortune, his cashier came by" — he pointed to the farmer — "and received five nobles from me in ready cash. I, being very desirous to try my luck further, played on; and as the dice, not being bound as an apprentice to him or any man (and thus forced to favor him), favored me, I drew a hand and won a hundred marks. Now I refer it to your judgments, whether the Friar is to seek his winnings."

The disguised King Edward I could see that the farmer had attempted to cheat the Friar of five nobles, and so he ruled, "By the Virgin Mary, Friar, the farmer must and shall pay you honestly before he passes by you."

"Shall I, sir?" the farmer said. "Why, will you be content to pay half, as you promised me?"

The disguised King Edward I had promised to repay all the money if the farmer were robbed, but the farmer — being guilty of fraud — would have happily accepted half.

The disguised King Edward I answered, "Aye, farmer, if you had been robbed of it; but if you are a gambler, I'll take no responsibility for your losses."

The farmer said, "Alas, I am ruined!"

The farmer gave Friar Hugh ap David the money and exited.

Llewelyn, who had been quietly watching the scene, said, "So, Sir Friar, now you have gathered up your winnings, I ask you to stand up and give the travelers their orders, so that Robin Hood may receive his toll."

Friar Hugh ap David said, "And I shall, my lord. Our thrice-renowned Llewelyn, Prince of Wales and Robin Hood of the great mountain, wills and commands all passengers, at the sight of my staff Richard, servant to me, Friar

David ap Tuck, to lay down their weapons, and quietly to yield, for taxes towards the maintenance of his highness' wars, half of all such gold, silver, money, and valuable possessions, as the said traveler has then about him; and if he conceals any part or parcel of the same, then he shall forfeit all that he possesses at that present. And this sentence is irrevocable, confirmed by our lord Llewelyn, who is Prince of Wales and Robin Hood of the great mountain."

Richard was the name the Friar had given his walking-staff.

Llewelyn said, "So surrender your wallets to Robin of the mountain."

He then said to the disguised King Edward I, "But who are you who disdains to pay this tax, as if you scorn the greatness of the Prince of Wales?"

The disguised King Edward I replied, "Truly, Robin, you seem to be a good fellow. There's my bag of money; half is mine, and half is yours. But let's fight, if you dare, man for man, to see who shall have the whole bag of money. If you win, you get the whole bag of money. If I win, I get the whole bag of money."

Llewelyn said, "Why, you speak as you should speak."

The disguised King Edward I spoke like a man, impressing Llewelyn.

Llewelyn then said to the others present, "My masters, on pain of my displeasure, depart this place, and leave us two to ourselves. I must lop his longshanks, before I'll ear to a pair of longshanks."

By "ear," he meant bow so low that his ears were near his opponent's long legs.

The disguised King Edward I said, "They are fair marks — valuable coins — sir, and I must defend them as I may.

"Davy, leave."

Davy was the disguised Sir David.

The disguised King Edward I then said, "Hold here, my hearts. Long-legs gives you this among you to spend blows one with another."

He threw the moneybag on the ground between Llewelyn and himself. They were the "hearts" who would fight over the money.

Friar Hugh ap David and Rice ap Meredith exited with the prisoners.

Sir David said to himself, "Now Davy's days have almost come at an end."

There was a strong possibility that the disguised King Edward I would defeat and kill Llewelyn. If that would happen, Sir David's life would become harder.

Sir David exited.

Mortimer, still disguised as a potter, said to himself, "But, Mortimer, this sight is strange. Stay out of sight in some corner to see what will happen in this battle."

He withdrew and watched.

King Edward I removed part of his disguise and said, "Now, Robin of the Wood, alias Robin Hood, be it known to your worship by my words that the longshanks that you aim at have brought the King of England into these mountains to see Llewelyn and to crack a blade with this man who supposes himself to be Prince of Wales."

King Edward I now regarded his newborn son and not Llewelyn as the lawful Prince of Wales.

"What, Sir King!" Llewelyn said. "Welcome to Cambria. What, foolish Edward, do you dare to endanger yourself to travel in these mountains? Are you so foolhardy as to combat with the Prince of Wales?"

King Edward I said, "What I dare, you can see for yourself; what I can perform, you shall shortly know. I think you are a gentleman, and therefore I do not scorn to fight with you."

Gentlemen were willing to fight each other, but they would refuse to fight a lowly born man.

Llewelyn said, "Edward, I am as good a man as yourself."

"That I shall try and test if it is really so," King Edward I said.

They fought. Sir David returned and fought on the side of his brother Llewelyn. Seeing that, Mortimer fought on the King's side.

Seeing Sir David, King Edward I said, "Hallo, Edward! How are your senses confounded!"

He then said, "What, Davy, is it possible that you are false and disloyal to the King of England?"

Sir David, who had been spying for his brother Llewelyn while pretending to be loyal to King Edward I, said, "Edward, I am true to Wales, and I have been friends with Wales since my birth, and that shall the King of England know to his cost."

Llewelyn said to the still-disguised Mortimer, "What, potter, didn't I order you to be gone with your fellows?"

Removing part of his disguise, Mortimer said, "Traitor, I am no potter. I am Mortimer, the Earl of March, whose purpose in coming to these woods is to deceive you and take away from you your love: Lady Eleanor. And I held myself ready to save my sovereign's life."

"Upon them, brother!" Sir David said to Llewelyn. "Let them not rest."

All four men fought.

King Edward defeated Llewelyn and had him at his mercy, and Sir David defeated Mortimer and had him at his mercy.

King Edward I said to Llewelyn, "Villain, you die! God and my right have prevailed."

Sir David said to Mortimer, "Base Earl! Now David triumphs in your overthrow."

He then looked at King Edward I and Llewelyn and said, "Damn! Llewelyn is at the feet of Longshanks!"

King Edward I looked at Mortimer and Sir David and said, "What! Mortimer is under the sword of such a traitor!"

Willing to die for his King, Mortimer said, "Brave King, run your sword up to the hilts into the blood of the rebel Llewelyn."

King Edward I replied, "Oh, Mortimer, your life is dearer to me than millions of rebels!"

"Edward, release my brother, and Mortimer lives," Sir David said.

King Edward I replied, "Aye, villain, you know too well how dearly I regard my Mortimer."

He said to Llewelyn, "Rise, man, and assure yourself that the hate I bear to you is love in comparison to the deadly hatred I bear to that notorious rebel — your brother, Sir David."

Mortimer said to King Edward I, "Let's leave! His sight to me is like the sight of a cockatrice."

A cockatrice is a mythological monster that can kill someone by looking at him or her.

Mortimer said to Sir David, "Villain, I go to revenge myself on your treason, and to make you an example to the world of mountainous treason, falsehood, and ingratitude."

King Edward I and Mortimer exited.

Sir David said, "Brother, he chafes, but hard was your luck to be overmastered by the coward."

"He is no coward, David," Llewelyn said. "His courage is similar to the courage of a lion, and were it not that rule and sovereignty set us against each other, I could love and honor the man for his valor."

"But the potter!" Sir David said about Mortimer. "Oh, the villain will never go out of my mind while I live! He will never leave my thoughts, and I will devise a way to be revenged on his villainy."

Llewelyn replied, "Well, David, what will be shall be; therefore, casting these matters out of our heads, David, I say that you are welcome to Cambria. Let us go in and be merry after this cold cooling, and let us prepare to strengthen ourselves against the latest threats."

CHAPTER 13

At Carnarvon Castle in Wales, the newborn baby had been christened Edward, and Gloucester and Joan had been married. Heralds were present, and two noblemen — Edmund Duke of Lancaster and the Earl of Sussex — attended on Joan. A Bishop was also present.

Gloucester said, "Welcome, Joan, Countess of Gloucester, to Gilbert de Clare forever!"

The name of the Earl of Gloucester was Gilbert de Clare.

The Earl of Sussex said, "God give them joy!

"Cousin Gloucester, let us now go visit the King and Queen, and present their majesties with their young son: Edward Prince of Wales."

They went to King Edward I's pavilion; the King was sitting in his tent, with his pages present.

The Bishop said, "We here present your highness most humbly with your young son: Edward of Carnarvon, Prince of Wales."

Trumpets sounded.

All said, "God save Edward of Carnarvon, Prince of Wales."

King Edward I said, "Edward, Prince of Wales, God bless you with long life and honor!"

He kissed his son.

He said to Joan, "Welcome, Joan, Countess of Gloucester! God bless you and yours forever!"

He kissed her.

He then said, "Lords, let us visit my Queen and wife, whom we will at once present with a son and daughter honored to her desire."

Trumpets sounded, and they marched to Queen Eleanor's chamber. She lay in her bed.

The Bishop said, "We humbly present your majesty with your young son, Edward of Carnarvon, Prince of Wales."

Trumpets sounded.

All present said, "God save Edward of Carnarvon, Prince of Wales."

Queen Eleanor kissed the Prince and said, "Many thanks, Bishop."

She gave him a purse of money and said, "Here, take that to buy yourself a rochet."

A rochet is an ecclesiastical vestment that Bishops wear.

She said to her son, "Welcome, Welshman."

She then said, "Here, nurse, open the front of his clothing and hold him close to the fire to warm him, for God's sake; they have touzled him, and they have washed him thoroughly by dunking him in the baptismal fount, and that is good."

"To touzel" means "to handle roughly."

She then said:

"And welcome, Joan, Countess of Gloucester! God bless you with long life, honor, and heart's-ease!

"I am now as good as my word, Earl of Gloucester: She is yours. Make much of her, gentle Earl.

King Edward I said, "Now, my sweet Nell, what more commands my Queen, so that nothing may be lacking to make perfect her contentment?"

"Nothing, sweet Ned," Queen Eleanor said, "but please, my King, feast the lords and ladies royally."

She said to the people around her, "And thanks a thousand times, good men and women, to you all for this duty and honor done to your Prince."

King Edward I said to Gloucester, "Master bridegroom, by old custom this is your waiting-day."

This was his day to wait on and attend to his new wife.

King Edward I then said:

"Brother Edmund, revel it now or never for honor of your England's son.

"Gloucester, now, like a splendid bridegroom, marshal this group of people, and set these lords and ladies to dancing; so shall you fulfill the old English proverb, 'It is merry in hall when beards wag all.'"

The beards would waggle with laughter.

The lords and ladies danced, and then they, with the King and Queen, sat down.

Versses entered the scene with a halter — a noose — around his neck. He was delivering the message from King John Baliol of Scotland.

Recognizing Versses, King Edward I asked, "What tidings does Versses bring to our court?"

Versses replied, "Tidings to make you tremble, English King."

"Me tremble, boy!" King Edward I said. "No news from Scotland can even once make English Edward stand aghast."

Versses said, "Baliol has chosen at this time to stir — to rouse himself like a lion and cast off the yoke that the Scots ingloriously have borne from you and all the predecessors of your line. And he will make his inroads into your country to re-obtain his right to rule autonomously, and for his homage to you, he sends you this despite."

The "despite" was the noose Versses was wearing, in addition to the words of defiance.

Edmund Duke of Lancaster said, "Why, how is it now, princox! Do thou prate to a King?"

The word "princox" means "impertinent fellow."

Versses said, "I deliver my message truly from my King. This sword and target [small shield] chide and reprove in louder terms. I bring defiance from King John Baliol of Scotland to English Edward and all his barons."

King Edward I said, "By the Virgin Mary, so I think, thou defy me with a vengeance."

Versses said, "Baliol, my King, in Berwick makes his court. His military camp he spreads upon the sandy plain and dares you to come to battle as is his right."

Edmund Duke of Lancaster said, "What! Court and camp in Englishmen's despite?"

King Edward I said to Versses, "Wait, messenger: Commend me to your King: Wear around your neck my gold chain, and carry this message to him."

The gold chain was a valuable gift. The chain was a necklace that could be worn with honor by males.

King Edward I then told Versses the message: "Greet all his rout of rebels, both greater and lesser in social status. Tell them such shameful end will hit them all: They will all be hanged. Proceed with this message as resolutely back as thou brought to England your Scottish insults.

"Tell Baliol, then, disdainfully from us that we'll rouse him from his hold, and make him soon dislodge his camp and we will capture his walled town.

"Say what I bid you to say, Versses, to his teeth and to his face, and earn this favor and a better thing."

By delivering the message, Versses would earn the gold chain. A "better thing" could be the favor of King Edward I. That favor could be valuable indeed once the Scottish forces were defeated.

Versses, who had delivered the defiant Scottish message under duress, replied, "Yes, King of England, whom my heart beloves: Know that as I promised John Baliol to bravely defy you here, so shall I deliver to John Baliol this challenge from you. I shall bid him base from you."

He was referring to a children's game called Prisoner's Bars or Prisoners' Base. Children would divide into two teams, and members of one team would try to catch and imprison members of the other team who ventured out of their home base, aka home territory. "To bid base" meant "to challenge to a pursuit." Baliol had challenged King Edward I basely, and now King Edward I was returning the challenge and the insult.

King Edward I said, "So shall thou earn my chain and favor, Versses. And carry to him this token — the noose — that thou delivered."

Verrses exited.

King Edward I said, "Why, now is England's harvest ripe."

He was looking forward to fighting the Scots.

He continued, "Barons, now may you reap the rich renown and fame that under warlike colors springs in the battlefield, and grows where banners wave upon the plains."

By fighting bravely in battles where colorful banners waved, the barons could gain a reputation for bravery.

King Edward I then said, "False, disloyal Baliol, Berwick is no proven stronghold that will shroud you from the strength of Edward's arm. No, Scot; your treason's fear shall make the breach for England's pure renown to enter in."

He believed that Berwick would definitely fall to the English army.

All present shouted, "At full speed, fall upon these treacherous Scots! At full speed, say all, fall upon these treacherous Scots!"

King Edward I said, "While we with Edmund, Gloucester, and the rest, with speedy journeys gather up our forces, and beat these insulting Scots away from England's boundaries, you, Mortimer, shall take the rebels in task who revel here and spoil fair Cambria. You will quell the rebellion here in Wales.

"My Queen, when she is strong and able to walk readily, shall travel to London and remain and refresh herself there.

"Then God shall send us happily all to meet, and enjoy the honors of our victories.

"Take the advantage of our foes and see the time, keep always our stronghold, our fight is yet on the plain.

"Baliol, I come — proud Baliol and ingrate —

"Prepared to chase your men from England's gate."

CHAPTER 14

Baliol and his train of attendants were at Berwick.

Comparing his listeners to oxen, Baliol said, "Princes of Scotland and my loving friends, whose necks are exhausted with the yoke of and servile bondage to these Englishmen, lift up your horns, and with your strong hoofs kick at the honor of your enemies. It is not ambitious thoughts of private rule that have forced your King to take on him these arms: It is our country's cause; it is the common good of us and of our brave posterity. To arms! To arms!

"Versses by this time has told King Edward I our minds, and he has defied proud England to the utmost. We will remunerate Versses' resolution with gold, with glory, and with kingly gifts."

The First Lord said, "By sweet Saint Jerome, Versses will not spare anything when telling his message to the English King, and he will beard the jolly Longshanks to his face, even if Longshanks were the greatest monarch in the world."

To figuratively "beard" a man was to insult him. The literal meaning was to pull another man's beard.

The First Lord continued, "And here Versses comes. His noose makes him hasten here."

Versses entered the scene.

Versses said to Baliol, "Long live my lord, the rightful King of Scots."

Baliol replied, "Welcome, Versses! What is the news from England? Is it similar — defiant — to the message that Scotland's King — me — sent the King of England?"

Referring to himself in the third person, Versses said, "Versses, my lord, speaking terms appropriate to himself, like to the messenger of the Scottish King, defied the peers of England and her lords, so that all his barons trembled at my threats, and Longshanks himself, just as daunted and amazed, gazed on my face, not knowing what to say, until rousing up he shook his threatening hair.

"'Versses,' said he, 'take for yourself King Edward's chain, upon condition that you take a message to Baliol, false perjured Baliol' — for in these terms he

"

told me to greet your grace, and he gave this noose to your excellence. I took the chain, and I give your grace the rope. "

Angry, Baliol said, "You took the chain, and you give my grace the rope!"

He ordered, "Lay hold of him and arrest him."

He then said to Versses, "Why, miscreate recreant — misshapen traitor — do you dare to bring a noose to your King? But I will reward your pains, and in that chain upon a silver gallows shall you hang, so that honored with a golden rope of England, and a silver gibbet of Scotland, you may hang in the air for fowls to feed upon, and men to wonder at."

Once dead, the hanged man would stay hanging from the noose for several days.

Baliol ordered, "Away with him! Take him away!"

CHAPTER 15

Somewhere in Wales, Mortimer and his soldiers were pursuing the rebels.

Mortimer shouted, "Strike up that drum!

"Follow, pursue, and chase!

"Follow, pursue!

"Spare not the proudest man who havocs and lays waste to England's sacred royalty!"

War trumpets sounded.

CHAPTER 16

At Carnarvon Castle in Wales, Queen Eleanor was alone.

She said to herself, "Now is a suitable time to purge our melancholy and be revenged upon this London dame."

The London dame was Mary, the Mayoress of London.

Queen Eleanor called for her attendant: "Katherina!"

Katherine entered the room and said, "I am here, madam."

Queen Eleanor ordered, "Bring our Mayoress here."

Katherine said, "I will, madam."

She exited.

Queen Eleanor said to herself, "Now, Nell, think of some tortures for the dame and then purge your anger to the utmost."

The Mayoress returned with Katherine.

Queen Eleanor said, "Now, Mistress Mayoress, you have asked to attend on me, and therefore to reward your courtesy, our mind is to bestow an office on you immediately."

The office was a job with a title.

The Mayoress replied politely, "I myself, my life, and my service, mighty Queen, are humbly at your majesty's command."

Queen Eleanor said, "Then, Mistress Mayoress, say whether you will be our nurse or our laundress?"

As nurse, the Mayoress would expect to take care of baby Edward Prince of Wales.

If the Mayoress were lactating, she could be a wet nurse to baby Edward: She could breastfeed him.

The Mayoress said, "Then may it please your majesty to employ your handmaid — your servant, me — as your nurse. She will attend the cradle carefully."

Queen Eleanor replied, "Oh, no, nurse; the babe needs no great rocking — it can lull itself."

She ordered, "Katherina, bind her in the chair, and let me see how she will become a nurse."

Katherina bound the Mayoress to the chair.

"Good," Queen Eleanor said. "Now, Katherine, draw forth her breast, and let the serpent suck his fill."

Katherina uncovered the Mayoress' breast, took a poisonous snake from a basket, and applied it to the Mayoress' breast.

"Why, good," Queen Eleanor said. "Now she is a nurse."

She then said to the poisonous snake, "Suck on, sweet babe."

The Mayoress pleaded:

"Ah, Queen, sweet Queen, seek not my blood to spill,

"For I shall die before this adder have his fill!"

Queen Eleanor said, "Whether you die or don't die, my mind is fully pleased."

She then ordered:

"Come, Katherina. To London now will we,

"And leave our Mayoress with her nursery."

Katherine said, "Farewell, sweet Mayoress, look after the babe."

Queen Eleanor and Katherine exited.

The Mayoress of London said, "Farewell, proud Queen, the author of my death, the scourge of England and the scourge to English dames!

"Ah, husband, sweet John Bearmber, Mayor of London, ah, if you knew how your wife Mary is perplexed, soon would you come to Wales, and rid me of this pain.

"But, oh, I die! My wish is all in vain."

She died.

CHAPTER 17

At Irfon Bridge in Wales, Llewelyn was running away from Mortimer and the English soldiers.

He said, "The angry heavens frown on Britain's woe to eclipse the glory of fair Cambria. With sour aspects the dreadful planets frown."

The stars were against Llewelyn, and his luck was bad.

He continued:

"Llewelyn, shall you basely turn your back and fly [flee]?

"No, Welshmen fight it out to the last and die.

"For if my men safely have got the bride, heedless of fortune, I'll take no notice of any bad event.

"England's broad womb hasn't got that armed band of soldiers who can expel Llewelyn from his land."

As long as his bride — Lady Eleanor — was safe, he could bear whatever bad fortune came his way.

Sir David, running from the English soldiers, entered the scene. He was carrying a noose and was ready to hang himself.

He said, "Flee, Lord of Cambria! Flee, Prince of Wales! Sweet brother, flee! The battlefield is won by the English and lost by us! You are beset by England's furious troops, and cursed Mortimer, like a lion, leads them. Our men have gotten the bridge, but all in vain. The Englishmen are now upon our backs. Either flee or die, for Edward has won the day.

"As for me, I have my rescue in my hand. England shall inflict no torments on me.

"Farewell, Llewelyn, until we meet in Heaven."

Sir David exited, and four English soldiers entered the scene.

The First Soldier ordered, "Follow, pursue!"

Seeing but not recognizing Llewelyn, he said, "Lie there, whoever you are."

He killed Llewelyn with a pike-staff.

Looking closer at Llewelyn, he said, "But wait, my hearts!"

His "hearts" were his fellow soldiers.

He added, "Let us his countenance see. This is the Prince: Llewelyn. I know him by his face.

"Oh, gracious fortune that made me so fortunate to spoil the weed that chokes fair Cambria! Drag him away from here, and in this bushy wood bury his corpse; but as for his head, I vow I will present our governor — Mortimer —with it."

The head was proof of Llewelyn's death. As the soldier who had killed Llewelyn, English's enemy, the First Soldier would receive a rich reward.

CHAPTER 18

Near Irfon Bridge in Wales, Friar Hugh ap David stood. He had placed a noose about his neck.

He said to his pike-staff, "Come, my gentle Richard, my true servant, that in some storms have stood by your master. May you hang, I plead to you, lest I hang for you."

Friar Hugh ap David knew that the Welsh had lost the battle and that Mortimer, if he wished not to be merciful, could hang many Welshmen, including himself. Therefore, he was retiring from warfare and hanging up his weapon — his pike-staff — as knights did when they grew old and retired from warfare.

He said to himself, "Hang up your pike-staff and go down on your knee marrowbones, like a foolish fellow who has gone far astray, and ask forgiveness from God and King Edward for playing the hell-raiser and the rebel here in Wales."

He continued, "Ah, gentle Richard, many a hot breakfast have we been at together!"

The hot breakfasts were hot fights.

He continued, "And now since, like one of the frozen-by-age knights of Mars, god of war, I must hang my weapon upon this tree, and come *per misericordiam* — appealing to pity — to the mad potter Mortimer, wring your hands, Friar, and sing a pitiful farewell to your pike-staff at parting."

Old soldiers often hung their weapons in a church as a votive offering.

Friar Hugh ap David sang his farewell to his pike-staff, hung it on a tree branch, and then exited.

CHAPTER 19

— SCENE XIX —

Near Irfon Bridge, Wales, the victorious Mortimer stood with his soldiers, including the soldier who had killed Llewelyn. Sir David was held captive. In addition, Lady Eleanor was in the custody of the English.

Mortimer ordered, "Bind fast the traitor — Sir David — and take him away so that the law may justly pass sentence upon him, and so that he may receive the reward of monstrous treasons and villainy, stain to the name and honor of his noble country!"

He said to the soldier who had killed Llewelyn, "The King shall reward your fortune and chivalry."

He then said to Lady Eleanor, "Sweet lady, don't hang your head and so heavenly looks down to the ground. God and the King of England have honor for you in store, and Mortimer's heart is at your service and at your commandment."

Lady Eleanor replied, "Thanks, gentle lord; but, alas, who can blame Eleanor for accusing her stars and lamenting her bad fortune, Eleanor who in one hour has lost both honor and happiness?"

Mortimer said, "And in one hour your ladyship may recover both, if you permit yourself to be advised by your friends."

Friar Hugh ap David, still wearing the noose, which was an acknowledgement that Mortimer had power of life and death over him, entered the scene and knelt before Mortimer.

Mortimer asked, "But what is the Friar doing here, kneeling upon his knee marrowbones?"

Friar Hugh ap David pleaded:

"Oh, potter, potter, the Friar does sue,

"Now his old master is slain and gone, to have a new."

The Friar wanted to serve King Edward I (thus saving his life) now that Llewelyn was dead.

Lady Eleanor said to herself, "Ah, sweet Llewelyn, how your death I rue!"

"Well said, Friar!" Mortimer said. "Better once than never. Give me your hand."

Mortimer raised the Friar from his kneeling position, thereby showing that he would grant the request.

He then said, "My cunning shall fail me, but we will be fellows yet; and now that Robin Hood is gone, it shall cost me hot water but you shall be King Edward's man."

Mortimer was joking that his being merciful to the Friar might get him in hot water.

He added, "Only I make this restriction on you — come not too near the fire, but, good Friar, be at my hand."

In this culture, "fire" could mean "vagina."

Mortimer was telling Friar Hugh ap David not to come too near Lady Eleanor.

Friar Hugh ap David replied, "Oh, sir; no, sir, it will not be so, sir. He — I — was warned about that very recently. I love none of that flesh."

Mortimer said, "Come on. And for those who have made their submission and given their names, in the King's name I pronounce their pardons; and so God save King Edward I."

CHAPTER 20

At Charing Green, a village west of London, Queen Eleanor and Joan stood. Thunder sounded and lightning flashed.

Queen Eleanor said, "Why, Joan, is this the welcome that the clouds give us? How dare these disturb our thoughts, knowing that I am Edward's wife and England's Queen, here thus to threaten me on Charing Green?"

Joan said, "Ah, mother, don't blaspheme so! Your blaspheming and other wicked deeds have caused our God to terrify your thoughts. And call to mind your sinful deed committed against the Mayoress here of lovely London. A better Mayoress of London was never bred — she was so full of mercy and pity to the poor. Her you have made away with and killed, and so London cries for vengeance on your head."

Queen Eleanor said, "I did not get rid of her; I did not kill her. By Heaven I swear, those who say I killed the Mayoress are traitors to Edward and to England's Queen."

Joan said, "Take heed, sweet lady-mother, don't swear like that: A field of delicious prized corn will not stop the mouths of those who say you have killed that virtuous woman."

Queen Eleanor said, "Gape, earth, open up and swallow me, and let my soul sink down to hell, if I were the author of that woman's tragedy!"

The earth opened up and swallowed her.

As the earth swallowed Queen Eleanor, she cried, "Oh, Joan, help! Joan, your mother sinks!"

Joan cried, "Oh, mother! My help is worthless!

"Oh, she has sunk, and here the earth is newly closed up again.

"Ah, Charing Green, forever change your hue, and may the grass never grow green again, but instead wither and return to stones, because beauteous Eleanor sank on you!

"Well, I will send to the King my father's grace, and inform him of this strange calamity."

CHAPTER 21

— SCENE XXI —

A battle was occurring at Montrose, a town on the coast of Scotland. The battle lasted a long time, but King Edward I and his soldiers triumphed. He and his train of attendants and his soldiers now held Baliol captive.

King Edward I said to Baliol, "Now, faithless, treacherous King, what are the fruits of insulting boasts? What end has treason but a sudden fall? Such people as have known your life and bringing up, have praised you for your learning and your knowledge. How comes it, then, that thou forgot your books that schooled you to forget ingratitude? Ingratitude is unnatural and unkind! This hand of mine anointed you and made you a King. This tongue of mine pronounced the decision of the mercy shown to you.

"If thou, in place of my unfeigned love, have levied arms in order to attempt to seize my crown, see now the fruits of your attempt: Your glories are dispersed and dissipated, and like a heifer, since thou have passed your boundaries and made inroads into England, your sturdy neck must stoop to bear this yoke."

Baliol replied, "I learned this lesson, Edward, from my books: To keep a just equality of mind and an even temperament and be content with every fortune — good or bad — as it comes. So thou can threaten me with no more than I expect."

King Edward I said, "So, sir: Your moderation is forced. You are forced to accept whatever happens to you now because you have no other choice. Your goodly glosses — pretty words — cannot make your bad fortune good."

Baliol said, "Then will I keep in silence what I mean, since Edward thinks my meaning is not good."

King Edward I said, "Nay, Baliol, speak forth, if there yet remains in you a little remnant of persuading art."

He was willing to hear what Baliol had to say to him.

Baliol said, "If cunning words may have power to win the King, let those employ them who can flatter him. If honored deed may reconcile the King, it lies in me to give and him to take."

Baliol was rejecting flattering the King in order to save his life, but he was willing to do a deed for the King that would save his life.

King Edward I said, "Why, what remains for Baliol now to give?"

Baliol replied, "Allegiance, as becomes a royal King."

King Edward I said, "What league of faith can there be where league is broken once?"

Baliol had previously sworn allegiance to King Edward I, but Baliol had broken his oath of allegiance. Why then should King Edward trust any oath of allegiance that Baliol made now?

Baliol said, "The greater hope in them who once have fallen."

Having rebelled and had his rebellion broken, a rebel would have learned his lesson.

King Edward I said, "But foolish are those monarchs who yield a conquered realm upon submissive vows."

Baliol said, "There, take my crown, and so redeem my life."

Baliol no longer needed to be King of Scotland, if giving up the kingdom meant that he could save his life.

King Edward I said, "Aye, sir; that was the better choice of the two.

"For whoever quells the pomposity of haughty, proud minds and breaks the staff — the army — on which they build their trust, can be sure that if the rebels lack power, they can do no harm.

"Baliol shall live; but yet within such bounds that, if his wings grow enough for flight, they may be clipped."

Baliol would live, but he would live without power. He would also be watched to ensure that he did not grow ambitious again.

CHAPTER 22

— SCENE XXII —

At Potter's Hive, near Charing Green, where Queen Eleanor sank into the ground, the Potter's Wife and John, her servant, talked together. They were near a quay used by ships that carried goods to London. Thunder sounded and lightning flashed.

The Potter's Wife said, "John, let's go. You move as though you slept. You are a great big knave and yet you are afraid of a little thundering and lightning!"

John replied, "Do you call this a little thundering? I am sure my breeches find it a great deal, for I am sure they are stuffed with thunder."

Well, stuffed with something, anyway.

The Potter's Wife said, "They are stuffed with a fool, aren't they? Will it please you to carry the lantern a little handsomer so we can see better, and not to carry it with your hands in your slops?"

Slops are trousers.

John replied, "Slops, say you! I wish I had tarried at home by the fire, and then I should not have any need to put my hands in my pockets! But I'll bet my life I know the reason for this foul weather."

"Do you know the reason?" the Potter's Wife said. "Please, John, tell me, and let me hear this reason."

John said, "I bet my life some of your gossips that we just came from are cross-legged, but you are 'wise,' mistress, for you come now away, and will not stay a-gossiping in a dry house all night."

Sitting cross-legged was supposed to bring bad luck. Such posture was also thought to be used in sorcery.

The Potter's Wife asked, "Would it please you to walk and leave off your knavery?"

Queen Eleanor slowly rose out of the earth.

"But wait, John," the Potter's Wife said. "What's that which is rising out of the ground? Jesus bless us, John! Look how it rises higher and higher!"

"By my faith, mistress, it is a woman," John said. "Good Lord, do women grow? I never saw one grow before."

He was comparing Queen Eleanor to a growing plant.

"Hold your tongue, you foolish knave," the Potter's Wife said. "It is the spirit of some woman."

Queen Eleanor said, "Huh, let me see! Where am I? On Charing Green? Aye, on Charing Green here, nearby Westminster Cathedral, where I was crowned, and Edward there made King.

"Aye, it is true; so it is, and therefore, Edward, don't kiss me, unless you will immediately perfume your lips and freshen your breath, Edward."

The Potter's Wife said, "*Ora pro nobis*!"

The Latin means, "Pray for us!"

She continued, "John, please, fall to your prayers.

"For my life, it is Queen Eleanor who chafes and frets thus — she who sunk this day on Charing Green, and now has risen up on Potter's Hive; and therefore truly, John, I'll go to her."

The Potter's Wife went to Queen Eleanor.

"Welcome, good woman," Queen Eleanor said. "What place is this? Sea or land? Please show it to me."

The Potter's Wife replied, "Your grace need not fear: You are on firm ground. This place is the Potter's Hive, and therefore cheer up, your majesty, for I will see you safely conducted to the court, if doing so would please your highness."

Queen Eleanor said, "Aye, good woman, conduct me to the court so that there I may bewail and lament my sinful life, and call to God to save my wretched soul."

A cry of "Westward ho!" sounded.

Queen Eleanor asked, "Woman, what noise is this I hear?"

The Potter's Wife said, "If it pleases your grace, the watermen are calling for passengers to go westward now."

Queen Eleanor replied, "That serves my purpose, for I will go immediately with them to King's-town to the court, and there I will rest until the King comes home. And therefore, sweet woman, conceal what thou have seen and lead me to those watermen, for here and now Eleanor droops."

She fainted.

Carrying the unconscious Queen to the quay, John said to her, "Come, come; this is a goodly leading of you, isn't it? First, you must make us afraid, and now I must be troubled with the carrying of you. I wish you were honestly laid in your bed, so that I were not troubled with you."

CHAPTER 23

King Edward, Edmund Duke of Lancaster, and some Lords were somewhere on the road to London from Scotland.

A messenger entered the scene and said, "May honor and fortune wait upon the crown of princely Edward, England's valiant King!"

King Edward I replied, "Thanks, messenger; and if my God grants that winged Honor attend upon my throne, I'll make her spread her plumes upon the heads of those whose true allegiance confirms, strengthens, and secures the crown."

He then asked, "What is the news in Wales? How goes our business there?"

The messenger replied, "The false disturber of that wasted soil, Llewelyn, with his adherents, was ambushed, my King. And in assurance he shall rebel no more, breathless he lies, and headless, too, my lords. These lines shall here unfold the details."

He handed King Edward I a letter.

King Edward I said, "A harmful weed, rooted out by wisdom, can never hurt the true engrafted plant."

Seeing Sir Thomas Spencer enter the scene, King Edward I said, "But what's the news Sir Thomas Spencer brings?"

"Wonders, my lord, wrapped up in homely words and letters to inform your majesty," Sir Thomas Spencer replied.

He gave the King some letters.

Reading the letters, King Edward I said, "Oh, heavens, what may these miracles portend? Nobles, my Queen is sick; but what is more —

"Read, brother Edmund, read about a wondrous occurrence."

He handed his brother a letter.

Edmund read out loud some lines about Queen Eleanor's sinking into the ground.

Edmund Duke of Lancaster said, "And I have neither heard nor read about so strange a thing before!"

King Edward I said, "Sweet Queen, this sinking is due to an excess of pride, with which your woman's heart did swell, a dangerous malady in the heart to dwell."

He then ordered, "Lords, we march towards London now in haste. I will go see my lovely Eleanor and comfort her after this strange affright. And because she is insistent to have secret conversation and conference with some Friars of France, Mun, you shall go with me, and I will go with you, and we will together take the sweet confession of my Nell. We will have French enough to parle with the Queen."

The King wanted his brother Edmund ("Mun") and himself to disguise themselves as French Friars and hear Queen Eleanor's confession. That way, they would find out what sins she had to repent. Such sins must be great because they had caused her to sink into the earth.

Edmund Duke of Lancaster said, "If I might advise your royal majesty, I would not go for millions of gold.

"Who knows, your grace, if you go disguised, what you may hear, in secrecy revealed, which may appall and discontent your highness?

"A goodly creature is your Eleanor, brought up in niceness and in delicacy. So then don't listen to her confession, lord, and wound your heart with some unkind ideas."

He said to himself, referring to himself, "And as for Lancaster, he may and must not go."

King Edward I replied, "Brother, I am resolved and determined to do this, and I will go, if God gives life, and cheer my dying Queen. Why, Mun, why, man, whatever King Edward hears, it lies in God and him to pardon all.

"I'll have no ghostly — religious — fathers out of France. England has learned clerics and confessors to comfort and absolve, as men may do, and I'll be a ghostly father for this once."

Edmund Duke of Lancaster said to himself, referring to himself:

"Edmund, you must not go, although you die:

"And yet how may you here your King deny?

"Edward is gracious, merciful, meek, and mild,

"But furious when he finds he is beguiled."

King Edward I ordered, "Messenger, hurry back to Shrewsbury, near Wales. Tell Mortimer, your master, to speed fast to London and with his good fortune welcome us to London. I long to see my beauteous lovely Queen."

CHAPTER 24

— SCENE XXIV —

At Shrewsbury, England were Mortimer and his officers (including a sheriff), Friar Hugh ap David, Jack, and Morgan Pigot the harper. Sir David stood on a hurdle (a kind of wooden panel) that would take him to his place of execution. Llewelyn's head was displayed on a spear.

Friar Hugh ap David, Jack the novice, and Morgan Pigot the harper had all been pardoned and were now on the side of the English.

"Keep moving," Friar Hugh ap David said. "Keep moving."

Jack the novice said, "Hold up your torches because they are dripping."

Friar Hugh ap David said, "This is a fair procession.

"Sir David, be of good cheer: You cannot go the wrong way because you have so many guides at hand."

Sir David would have preferred to go the wrong way.

"Be sure of that," Jack the novice said, "for we go on the highway all the way to the gallows, I assure you."

"I go where my star leads me, and die in my country's just cause and quarrel," Sir David said.

The star was the one that influenced his future and his fortune.

Morgan Pigot the harper said, "The star that twinkled at your birth, my good brother, has marred your mirth: An old often-said proverb is 'Earth must return to earth.'"

In other words, "Dust to dust."

He continued:

"Next year there will be a piteous dearth of hemp, I dare lay a penny,

"Because this year are hanged so many."

The ropes that hanged traitors were made of hemp.

Friar Hugh ap David said, "Well said, Morgan Pigot, harper and prophet for the King's own mouth."

Morgan Pigot the harper was now working for King Edward I.

Jack the novice said, "Tum date dite dote dum."

These were the musical sounds that Morgan Pigot the harper had made while foretelling Llewelyn's future.

Jack continued, "This is the day, the time is come: Morgan Pigot's prophecy, and Lord Llewelyn's tragedy."

Friar Hugh ap David said:

"Who says the prophet is an ass

"Whose prophecies come so to pass?

"Said he not often, and sung it, too,

"Llewelyn, after much ado,

"Should in spite heave up his chin

"And be the highest of his kin?

"And see, aloft Llewelyn's head,

"Impaled with a crown of lead!

"My lord, let not this soothsayer lack,

"Who has such cunning in his jack[et]."

Morgan Pigot the harper who had foretold Llewelyn's future, had said that "you must necessarily be advanced to be the highest position of your kin."

Now Llewelyn's head was held high, impaled on the top of a spear.

Morgan Pigot the harper said:

"Friar David, hold still your clack [chatter],

"Lest your heels make your neck crack."

His neck would crack when he was hanged and his heels stood on air.

Friar Hugh ap David replied, "Gentle prophet, if you love me, don't speak anything against me: It is the worst luck in the world to stir a witch or anger a wise man."

He then said, "Master Sheriff, can we go any faster? Best give my horses some more hay."

CHAPTER 25

At the Palace at Kingston-upon-Thames, Queen Eleanor was lying on her death-bed, attended by Joan and other ladies.

Queen Eleanor ordered, "Call forth those renowned Friars who have come from France —"

A lady exited to call the Friars.

She continued, "— and raise me, gentle ladies, higher in my bed, so that until this engine of my speech falters and I cease to utter my concealed guilt, I may confess and so repent my sins."

Joan asked, "What plague afflicts your royal majesty?"

Queen Eleanor replied, "Ah, Joan, I perish through a double-war!"

Her body was failing, and her conscience was guilty.

She continued:

"The first war is in this painful prison — my body — of my soul. A world of dreadful sins hole up there to fight, and nature, having lost her working power, is yielding up her earthly fortunes to death. Soon I will die, and my worldly affairs will come to a rest.

"Next my soul is oppressed by a second war, in that my conscience, which is loaded with misdeeds, sits seeing my ruin to ensue, without especial favor from above. Unless God forgives my sins, I will be damned."

Joan said, "Your grace must account it a warrior's cross, to make a defense where there is no danger."

Joan was trying to reassure her mother that she was not in danger of damnation. This was a warrior's cross, like those the Crusaders wore. Crusaders who died fighting in the Holy Land were martyrs who went directly to Paradise. Joan was saying that Queen Eleanor was like a Crusader-martyr and in no danger of damnation.

Joan continued, "Subdue your fever by precious art, and help yourself always through hope of heavenly aid."

The "precious art" could be the skill of a physician who could cure her fever, or perhaps it could be religious art — religious skill and knowledge — that would bring her spiritual comfort.

Queen Eleanor said, "The worry-free shepherds on the mountain's tops see the sailor and his ship floating on the surge of waves, and see the threatening winds come springing with the floods to overwhelm and drown his damaged keel. The sailor's ship-rigging is torn, and the ship's sails are borne overboard. How pale with fear, like yellow flowers, the Captain stands upon the hatches, waiting for the wave of the sea that will sink his ship. Wringing his hands that ought to work the pump, the Captain may blame his fear for his not laboring to save his life."

Like the ship Captain, Queen Eleanor was full of fear. To save her soul, she needed to confess her sins, but her body was paralyzed by pain — both physical and spiritual. Joan was like a worry-free shepherd who was safely on land.

Queen Eleanor continued, "So you, poor soul, may tell a servile tale of my sins, and you may counsel me, but I who am experiencing the pain may hear you talk but not repair my harm. But ghastly death already is addressed to glean and collect the final blossom of my life."

Would she live long enough to confess her sons?

She said, "My spirit fails me. Have these Friars come?"

The lady who had left to get the Friars returned. She brought with her King Edward I and his brother Edmund Duke of Lancaster, both of whom were disguised as French Friars.

The disguised King Edward I said, "*Dominus vobiscum*."

The Latin means, "May God be with you."

The disguised Edmund Duke of Lancaster said, "*Et cum spiritu tuo*."

The Latin means, "And with your soul."

Queen Eleanor said, "Draw near, grave and revered fathers, and approach my bed."

She ordered, "Leave our presence, ladies, for a while, and leave us to our private conversation."

Joan and the ladies exited.

The disguised King Edward I asked, "What reason has caused your royal majesty to call your servants — we two Friars — from their country's boundaries in order to attend your pleasure here in England's court?"

Queen Eleanor replied, "Don't you see, holy Friars, my estate — my weak body — heading toward my grave?"

The disguised Edmund Duke of Lancaster replied, "We see and sorrow for your pain, fair Queen."

Queen Eleanor said, "By these external signs of my defects, Friars, imagine my internal grief. My soul — ah, my wretched soul! — within this breast, is faint and despairs of trying to mount the heavens with wings of grace. A hundred by-flocking troops of sin accompany me and stop my passage to my wished-for dwelling in Paradise."

The disguised King Edward I said, "The nearer to Paradise, Eleanor, the greater hope of health eternally."

He slipped up by calling her "Eleanor." A Friar would not address a Queen that way.

He continued, "Do think it fit for you to impart your grief and confess your sins to us. We by our prayers and counsel should arm aspiring souls to scale the heavenly grace."

Queen Eleanor said, "Shame and remorse stop my course of speech."

The disguised King Edward I said, "Madam, you need not dread our conference. We two, by the order of the holy church, are both anointed to sacred secrecy. We will keep your confession secret."

Queen Eleanor said, "If I did not think — indeed, if I were not assured — that your wisdoms would be silent in that cause, no fear could make me betray myself. But, gentle fathers, I have thought it good not to rely upon these Englishmen, but on your truth and integrity, you holy men of France. So then, as you love your life and England's welfare, keep my confession secret from the King. The reason for this is that my story closely concerns him, whose love compared with my loose delights, frightens my heart with many sorrows."

The disguised Edmund Duke of Lancaster said, "My heart is filled with apprehension."

The disguised King Edward I said, "Be silent, fellow Friar."

Queen Eleanor said, "In pride of youth, when I was young and beautiful and attractive — in the King of England's sight, the day before that night his highness should possess the pleasure of my wedlock's bed, wretch and accursed monster as I was, his brother Edmund, who was beautiful and young, upon my bridal couch by my consent enjoyed the flower and favor of my love, and I became a traitress to my lord."

Edmund Duke of Lancaster, who was Edward's brother, had slept with her — with her consent — the night before she and King Edward I enjoyed their wedding night together.

King Edward I looked sorrowfully at his brother and said, "*Facinus scelus! Infandum nefas*! "

The Latin means, "A crime committed! An unspeakable sin!"

The Edmund Duke of Lancaster said, "Madam, because of your sickness and the weakness of your wits, it would be very good to think before you speak."

He did not want her to reveal such secrets as this, which would make his brother the King angry at him. Kings had the power to execute traitors, and such an act as Edmund's could be construed as treason.

Queen Eleanor said, "Good father, I am not so weak, but that, I know, my heart breaks to think upon the time. But why exclaims this holy Friar so? Oh, pray, then, for my faults, religious man!"

Friars, of course, want dying people to confess ALL their sins so that ALL their sins can be forgiven. Unconfessed sins can lead to damnation.

The disguised King Edward I said, "It is charity in men of my degree to sorrow for our neighbors' heinous sins. And, madam, although some promise love to you, and some promise zeal to Edmund, brother to the King, I pray to the heavens that you both may soon repent. But might it please your highness to proceed?"

It was Edmund who promised love to Eleanor, and it was Eleanor who promised zeal to Edmund.

Queen Eleanor said, "To this sin a worser does succeed; for Joan of Acre, the supposed child and daughter of my lord the English King, is basely born because her father is not noble. She was begotten by a Friar, at the time that I arrived in France.

"My friends, the King's only true and lawful son — and he is my hope, his son who should succeed him — is Edward of Carnarvon, who was recently born in Wales.

"Now all the scruples and misgivings of my troubled mind I sighing sound within your reverent ears.

"Oh, pray, for pity! Pray, for I must die. Remit and do not punish, my God, the folly of my youth! My groaning spirit attends your throne — your mercy-seat.

"Fathers, farewell; commend me to my King.

"Commend me to my children and my friends, and close my eyes, for death will have his due."

Having finished confessing her sins, Queen Eleanor died.

Closing her eyes, King Edward I said, "Blushing, I shut these your enticing lamps, the wanton baits that made me suck my poison.

"Pyropus' hardened flames have never reflected more hideous flames than from my breast arise."

Pyropus is an alloy of copper and a small amount of gold. When made into thin sheets of metal, it has a fiery-red color. Fiery-red was the color of the jealous anger and grief in King Edward's heart.

King Edward I continued, "What sin can be more vile to your dearest lord than these: Our daughter Joan is basely begotten of a priest, and Ned, my brother, is the sex-partner of my love!

"Oh, that those eyes that lightened Caesar's brain,

"Oh, that those looks that mastered Phoebus' brand,

"Or else those looks that stained Medusa's face,

"Should enshrine deceit, desire, and lawless lust!"

The eyes that lightened Caesar's brain and made him giddy were those of Cleopatra. She seduced Mark Antony and both of them committed suicide after being defeated by Octavian, Julius Caesar's adopted son and heir.

The looks that mastered Phoebus Apollo the Sun-god's firebrand were those of Clymene, with whom he fathered Phaëthon, who asked to drive Apollo's Sun-chariot. Phaëthon, doomed youth, was unable to control the stallions, and they ran wildly away with the Sun-chariot, wreaking havoc and destruction upon Humankind and the world. The King of the gods, Jupiter, saved Humankind and the world by throwing a thunderbolt at Phaëthon and killing him.

Medusa was a beautiful maiden with whom the sea-god Poseidon had sex in a temple of the virgin goddess Athena. Disgusted by this act of sacrilege, Athena turned Medusa's hair into snakes; in addition, Athena made Medusa into a monster — a Gorgon — with the result that anyone who looked into Medusa's eyes was turned to stone.

In all three cases, a woman was beautiful, but bad things happened to her and to males who were associated with her. King Edward was comparing Queen Eleanor to all three women. Of course, he was associated with Queen Eleanor and he had just learned of some bad things that had happened to him because of that association.

King Edward I continued, "Unhappy King, dishonored in your family!"

Taking off his Friar's robe and belt, he said, "Hence, feigned garments, but unfeigned is my grief."

The robe and belt were feigned because the King was not a Friar; he was using the garments as a disguise.

Edmund Duke of Lancaster said, "Dread Prince, my brother, if my vows of innocence will persuade you, I call to witness Heaven in my behalf. If zealous prayer might drive you from suspicion of me, I bend my knees and kneel before you, and I humbly beg for this request to be granted to me: that you will drive these alleged sins you have just heard about out of your mind.

"May good never happen in my life, my lord, if once I dreamed upon this damned deed of adultery with the Queen! But my deceased sister-in-law and your Queen, afflicted with incurable maladies and lacking patience because of her pain, grew lunatic and has revealed 'sins' that were never dreamed upon, let alone committed.

"To prove that this is true, let me say that the greatest men of all within their learned books do record that all extremes end in nothing but extremes."

He meant that the Queen's extreme physical pain had led her to other extremes: extreme mental pain and insanity.

Edmund Duke of Lancaster continued, "So then think and believe, oh, King, that her agony in death bereaved her of sense and memory at once, so that she spoke she knew neither how nor what."

King Edward I said, "Sir, sir, your highness would eagerly like to hide your faults by using cunning vows and fawning words to excuse you. And well thou may delude and fool these listening ears, yet thou shall never assuage and make this jealous heart hurt less no matter what cunning vows you make and fawning words you use.

"Traitor, your head shall ransom my disgrace."

He then invoked Nemesis, goddess of retribution. Her father was Erebus, goddess of darkness. King Edward I identified her also with jealous retribution.

"Daughter of darkness, whose accursed bower the poet alleged to lie at Avernus, where Cimmerian darkness obscures the Sun, dreaded Jealousy, afflict me not so sorely!"

Avernus, a volcanic crater near Cumae, Italy, was the location of one of the entrances to the Underworld. In his epic poem *Aeneid*, the poet Virgil placed there the scourges of Humankind.

According to Virgil, the entrance to the Land of the Dead was densely populated with Grief, Cares, Diseases, Old Age, Fear, Hunger, Poverty, Death, Hard Labor, Restless Sleep, Evil Joys, Hallucinations, and War. Here lived the Furies and Discord. A tree grew at the entrance to the Land of the Dead — a tree whose fruit was False Dreams. Also living at the entrance to the Land of the Dead were monsters: Centaurs, Scyllas, Briareus and his hundred hands, the Hydra, the Chimera, Gorgons, Harpies, and Geryon and his three bodies.

King Edward I continued, "Fair Queen Eleanor could never be so false to me —

"Aye, but she vowed these treasons at her death, a time not fit to fashion monstrous lies."

Deathbed confessions tend to be believed because the dying person would not lie because lying is a sin and could endanger that person's immortal soul.

King Edward I continued, "Ah, my ungrateful brother as thou art, couldn't my love — nay, more, couldn't the law — nay, further, couldn't the natural affection of family members for each other allure you enough to refrain from this incestuous sin?

"Get out from my sight!"

Edmund Duke of Lancaster exited.

King Edward I ordered his attendants who were outside the chamber, "Call Joan of Acre here."

He then said to himself, "The lukewarm spring of tears distilling from Edmund's eyes, his oaths, his vows, his reasons wrested with remorse from forth his breast — they are poisoned with suspicion.

"I wish that I could deem false those evil things that I find to be too true."

As he spoke to himself, Joan entered the chamber and said, "I come to know what England's King commands. I wonder why your highness greets me thus, with strange looks and unacquainted terms."

The "unacquainted terms" were the words the King had said to himself — she had overheard them as she walked over to her father.

King Edward I said, "Ah, Joan, this wonder necessarily must wound your breast, for it has nearly slain my wretched heart."

Joan said, "What! Is the Queen, my sovereign mother, dead? I am full of sorrow! Unhappy lady, I am afflicted with sorrow!"

King Edward I said, "The Queen is dead; yet, Joan, don't lament. Poor soul, you are guiltless of this deceit, you who have more cause to curse than to complain."

Joan said, "My dreadful soul, assailed with doleful speech, compels me to bow my knees to the ground and kneel, begging your most royal majesty to rid your woeful daughter of suspicion."

Worried by her father's words, Joan was afraid that she had been accused of committing some transgression.

King Edward I said, "Aye, daughter, Joan? Poor soul, you are deceived! The King of England is no scorned priest."

She had knelt before him as if she were going to make a confession to a priest. She was also deceived in thinking that Edward was her father.

Joan asked, "Wasn't the Lady Eleanor your spouse, and am not I the offspring of your loins?"

She was asking if she were legitimate.

King Edward I replied, "Aye, but when ladies wish to run astray and pleating leave their liege in princes' laps, the poor supposed father wears the horn."

Some Queens wish to have affairs and leave their illegitimate offspring, who are either in the line of succession or who are possible Queens when they marry, in the King's lap. In these cases, the King is a cuckold and wears the invisible horns that cuckolds are supposed to have growing on their heads.

The verb "pleat" means literally to intertwine or interlace three or more strands to form a plait. In the King's sentence, it means to figuratively intertwine or interlace three people sexually: the King, the Queen, and the Friar.

King Edward I then said, "Joan, thou are the daughter to a lecherous Friar. A Friar was your father, luckless Joan. Your mother in confession, avowed no less, and I, vile wretch that I am, sorrowfully heard no less than this confession."

Joan said, "What! Am I, then, a Friar's not nobly-born child? Presumptuous wretch that I am, why do I express warm regard for my King?"

If she were not the King's daughter and instead were the daughter of a Friar, she ought not to have the warm relationship with the King that she had enjoyed until now.

Joan continued, "How can I look my husband in the face? Why should I live since my reputation is lost?"

Referring to the clothing she was wearing, she said, "Go away, you luxurious clothing!"

She then said, "Leave me now, world's delight!"

She fell groveling on the ground.

King Edward I said:

"*L'orecchie abbassa, come vinto e staneo*

"*Destrier c'ha in boeca il fren, gli sproni al fianco, —*

He was quoting two lines from Canto XX, stanza 131, of the Italian epic poem *Orlando Furioso*, which was written by Lodovico Ariosto.

This is William Stewart Rose's translation:

"*Stands like tired courser, who in pensive fit,*

"*Hangs down his ears, controlled by spur and bit*"

In these lines, a character named Zembino is compared to an old horse. He had just lost a single combat and as a result he must ride with an old hag.

King Edward I seems to have meant that Joan cannot control her fate.

King Edward I then said:

"*O sommo Dio, come I giudicii umani*

"*Spesso offuscati son da un nembo oscuro!*"

He was quoting two lines from two lines from Canto X, stanza 15, of *Orlando Furioso*.

This is William Stewart Rose's translation:

"*Almighty God, how fallible and vain,*

"*Is human judgment, dimmed by clouds obscure!*"

King Edward I continued, "Hapless and wretched, lift up your heavy, sorrowful head. Curse not so much at this unhappy chance. Inconstant Fortune always will have her course."

Joan replied, "My King, my King, let Fortune have her course: Flee, my soul, and take a better course.

"Woe is me, from royal state I now am fallen!

"You purple springs of blood that wander in my veins, and were once accustomed to feed my heavy, sorrowful heart, now all at once act quickly, and pity me and stop your powers, and change your native course.

"Dissolve your lukewarm bloody streams to air, and cease to be, so that I may be no more."

She wanted her blood to dry up, thus killing her.

She continued, "Your curled locks, draw from this cursed head."

An ancient way of expressing grief was to tear one's hair.

She continued, "Abase her pomp, for Joan is basely born!"

"Abase her pomp" meant to ruin her ostentatious appearance.

She continued, "Ah, Gloucester, thou, poor Gloucester, has the wrong!"

He thought that he had married the daughter of a King, but he had not.

She continued, "Die, wretch! Hurry, death, for Joan has lived too long."

Joan suddenly died at the feet of the Queen's bed.

King Edward I said, "Revive, luckless lady. Don't grieve like this.

"In vain I speak, for she revives no more. Poor luckless soul, your own repeated moans have wrought your sudden and untimely death."

He called, "Lords, ladies, hurry here!"

The ladies with Gloucester and some lords came running.

King Edward I said, "Ah, Gloucester, have you come? Then I must now present a tragedy to you. Your Joan is dead. Yet don't grieve her fall: She was too basely born a spouse for such a Prince as you."

Referring to personified Death, Gloucester said, "Do you conspire, then, with the heavens to work my harms?

"Oh, sweet assuager and reliever of our mortal misfortunes, desired death, deprive me of my life, so that I in death may end my life and love!"

King Edward I said, "Gloucester, your King is a partner and a partaker of your heaviness and sorrows, although neither tongue nor eyes betrays his grief, for I have lost a flower as fair as yours, a love more dear, for Eleanor is dead.

"But since the heavenly divine will decrees that all things change and die in their predetermined time, be content, and bear in your breast your swelling grief, as necessarily I must bear mine.

"Your Joan of Acre and my Queen deceased shall have that honor as is befitting for their state.

"You peers of England, see in royal pomp that these breathless bodies are entombed immediately, with all colorful attire covered with black.

"Let Spanish steeds, as swift as fleeting wind, convey these princes to their funeral. Before them let a hundred mourners ride.

"In every place where the funeral stops for the night, rear up a cross in token of their worth, whereon fair Eleanor's picture shall be placed.

"Once arrived at London, near our palace-bounds, inter my lovely Eleanor, lately deceased. And, in remembrance of her royalty, erect a rich and stately carved cross, on which her statue shall with glory shine, and henceforth see that you call it Charing Cross because she was the chariest — the dearest — and the choicest Queen, who did always delight my royal eyes.

"There she will dwell in darkness while I die in grief."

Some messengers entered, and the King said, "But, wait! What tidings do these messengers bring?"

One of the messengers said, "Sir Roger Mortimer, with all success, as previously your grace by a message did command, is here at hand in order to present our highness with signs of his victory in Wales.

"And faithless Baliol, the Scots' accursed King, with fire and sword threatens Northumberland."

Baliol had escaped whatever restrictions King Edward I had placed on him and was again making inroads into England.

King Edward I said, "How one affliction calls another affliction over! First death torments me, then I feel disgrace! And false Baliol means to defy me, too. But I will find provision to resist them all. My constancy shall conquer death and shame."

Everyone except Gloucester exited.

He said to himself:

"Now, Joan of Acre, let me mourn your fall.

"By myself, here alone, now I sit down and sigh.

"Sigh, hapless Gloucester, for your sudden loss: Pale death, alas, has banished all your pride, your wedlock-vows! How often have I beheld your eyes, your looks, your lips, and every part — how nature strove in them to show her art, in shine, in shape, in color, and in comparison!

"But now has death, the enemy of love, stained and deformed the shine, the shape, the red, with pale and dimness, and my love is dead.

"Ah, dead, my love! Vile wretch, why am I living? So wills fate, and I must be contented.

"All pomp in time must fade, and grow to nothing.

"Wept I like Niobe, yet it profits nothing."

Niobe was proud because she had given birth to six sons and six daughters, and she boasted aloud, "I am more worthy of respect than the goddess Leto, who has given birth to only two children: the twins Apollo and Artemis." Leto's children were angry at the disrespect shown to their mother, and in one day they killed all of Niobe's children, shooting them with arrows. Niobe wept.

Gloucester finished:

"So then cease, my sighs, since I may not regain her,

"And woe to wretched death that thus has slain her!"

APPENDIX A: BRIEF HISTORICAL BACKGROUND

KING RICHARD I: 1189-1199

He was also known as Richard the Lionheart because of his military prowess as a leader and soldier. He was a Christian commander in the Third Crusade. As King, he spent little time in England. Much of his time was spent defending his lands in France. He also spent time in captivity.

KING JOHN: 1199-1216

He was also known as John Lackland because he lost the Duchy of Normandy and most of his lands in France. In 1215, he signed the Magna Carta. King John is a bad King in Robin Hood stories.

KING HENRY III: 1216-1272

Son of King John, he reigned for 56 years. At the beginning of his reign, much of England was controlled by the French Prince Louis (later King Louis VIII), but at the end of his reign, England was controlled by the King of England.

KING EDWARD I: 1272-1307

Edward Longshanks fought and defeated the Welsh chieftains, and he made his eldest son the Prince of Wales. He won victories against the Scots, and he brought the coronation stone from Scone to Westminster.

KING EDWARD II: 1307-deposed 1327

At the Battle of Bannockburn in 1314, the Scots defeated his army. His wife and her lover, Mortimer, deposed him. According to legend, he was murdered in Berkeley Castle by means of a red-hot poker thrust up his anus.

KING EDWARD III: 1327-1377

Son of King Edward II, he reigned for a long time — 50 years. Because he wanted to conquer Scotland and France, he started the Hundred Years War in 1338. King Edward III and his eldest son, Edward the Black Prince, won important victories against the French in the Battle of Crécy (1346) and the Battle of Poitiers (1356).

One of King Edward III's sons was John of Gaunt, first Duke of Lancaster.

Another of King Edward III's sons was Edmund of Langley, first Duke of York.

During his reign, the Black Death — the bubonic plague — struck in 1348-1350 and killed half of England's population.

KING RICHARD II: 1377-deposed 1399

King Richard II was the son of Edward the Black Prince. In 1381, Wat Tyler led the Peasants Revolt, which was suppressed. King Richard II sent Henry, Duke of Lancaster, into exile and seized Henry's estates, but in 1399 Henry, Duke of Lancaster, returned from exile and deposed King Richard II, thereby becoming King Henry IV. In 1400, King Richard II was murdered in Pontefract Castle, which is also known as Pomfret Castle.

HOUSE OF LANCASTER

KING HENRY IV: 1399-1413

Henry, Duke of Lancaster, was the son of John of Gaunt, who was the third son of King Edward III. He was born at Bolingbroke Castle and so was also known as Henry of Bolingbroke. Returning from exile in France to reclaim his estates, he deposed King Richard II. He spent the 13 years of his reign putting down rebellions and defending himself against those who would assassinate or depose him. The Welshman Owen Glendower and the English Percy family were among those who fought against him. King Henry IV died at the age of 45.

KING HENRY V: 1413-1422

The son of King Henry IV, King Henry V renewed the war with France. He and his army defeated the French at the Battle of Agincourt (1415) despite being heavily outnumbered. He married Catherine of Valoise, the daughter of the French King, but he died before becoming King of France. He left behind a 10-month-old son, who became King Henry VI.

KING HENRY VI: 1422-deposed 1461; briefly returned to the throne in 1470-1471

The Hundred Years War ended in 1453; the English lost all land in France except for Calais, a port city. After King Henry VI suffered an attack of mental illness in 1454, Richard, third Duke of York and the father of King Henry IV and King Richard III, was made Protector of the Realm. England suffered civil war after the House of York challenged King Henry VI's right to be King of England. In 1470, King Henry VI was briefly restored to the English throne. In 1471, he was murdered in the Tower of London. A short time previously, his son, Edward, Prince of Wales, had been killed at the Battle of Tewkesbury in

1471; this was the final battle in the Wars of the Roses. The Yorkists decisively defeated the Lancastrians.

King Henry VI founded both Eton College and King's College, Cambridge.

WARS OF THE ROSES

From 1455-1487, the Yorkists and the Lancastrians fought for power in England in the famous Wars of the Roses. The emblem of the York family was a white rose, and the emblem of the Lancaster family was a red rose. The Yorkists and the Lancastrians were descended from King Edward III.

HOUSE OF YORK

KING EDWARD IV: 1461-1483 (King Henry VI briefly returned to the throne in 1470-1471)

Son of Richard, third Duke of York, he charged his brother George, Duke of Clarence, with treason and had him murdered in 1478. After dying suddenly, he left behind two sons aged 12 and 9, and five daughters.

His surviving two brothers in Shakespeare's play *Richard III* are these: 1) George, Duke of Clarence. Clarence is the second-oldest brother; and 2) Richard, Duke of Gloucester, and afterwards King Richard III. Gloucester is the youngest surviving brother.

William Caxton established the first printing press in Westminster during King Edward IV's reign.

KING EDWARD V: 1483-1483

The eldest son of King Edward IV, he reigned for only two months, the shortest-lived monarch in English history. He was 13 years old. He and his younger brother, Richard, were murdered in the Tower of London. According to Shakespeare's play, their uncle, Richard, Duke of Gloucester, who became King Richard III, was responsible for their murders.

KING RICHARD III: 1483-1485

Brother of King Edward IV, Richard, the Duke of Gloucester, declared the two Princes in the Tower of London — King Edward V and Richard, Duke of York — illegitimate and made himself King Richard III. In 1485, Henry Tudor, Earl of Richmond, a descendant of John of Gaunt, who was the father of King Henry IV, defeated King Richard III at the Battle of Bosworth Field in Leicestershire. King Richard III died in that battle.

King Richard III's father was Richard Plantagenet, Duke of York. His mother was Cecily Neville, Duchess of York.

King Richard III's death in the Battle of Bosworth Field is regarded as marking the end of the Middle Ages in England.

A NOTE ON THE PLANTAGENETS

The first Plantagenet King was King Henry II (1154-1189). From 1154 until 1485, when King Richard III died, all English Kings were Plantagenets. Both the Lancaster family and the York family were Plantagenets.

Geoffrey Plantagenet, Count of Anjou, was the founder of the House of Plantagenet. Geoffrey's son, Henry Curtmantle, became King Henry II of England, thereby founding the Plantagenet dynasty. Geoffrey wore a sprig of broom, a flowering shrub, as a badge; the Latin name for broom is *planta genista*, and from it the name "Plantagenet" arose.

The Plantagenet dynasty can be divided into three parts:

1154-1216: The Angevins. The Angevin Kings were Henry II, Richard I (Richard the Lionheart), and John 1.

1216-1399: The Plantagenets. These Kings ranged from King Henry III to King Richard II.

1399-1485: The Houses of Lancaster and of York. These Kings ranged from King Henry IV to King Richard III.

BEGINNING OF THE TUDOR DYNASTY
KING HENRY VII: 1485-1509

When King Richard III fell at the Battle of Bosworth, Henry Tudor, Earl of Richmond, became King Henry VII. A Lancastrian, he married Elizabeth of York — young Elizabeth of York in Shakespeare's *Richard III* — and united the two warring houses, York and Lancaster, thus ending the Wars of the Roses. One of his grandfathers was Sir Owen Tudor, who married Catherine of Valoise, widow of King Henry V.

KING HENRY VIII: 1509-1547

King Henry VIII had six wives. These are their fates: "Divorced, Beheaded, Died, Divorced, Beheaded, Survived." He divorced his first wife, Catherine of Aragon, so that he could marry Anne Boleyn. Because of this, England divorced itself from the Catholic Church, and King Henry VIII became the head of the Church of England. King Henry VIII had one son and two daughters, all of whom became rulers of England: Edward, daughter of Jane

Seymour; Mary, daughter of Catherine of Aragon; and Elizabeth, daughter of Anne Boleyn.

KING EDWARD VI: 1547-1553

The son of Henry VIII and Jane Seymour, King Edward VI succeeded his father at the age of nine; a Council of Regency with his uncle, Duke of Somerset, styled Protector, ruled the government.

During King Edward VI's reign, Archbishop Thomas Cranmer wrote the 1549 Book of Common Prayer.

When King Edward VI died, Lady Jane Grey was proclaimed Queen, but she ruled for only nine days before being executed in 1554, aged 17. Mary, daughter of Catherine of Aragon, became Queen. She was Catholic, thus the attempt to make Lady Jane Grey, a Protestant, Queen.

QUEEN MARY I (BLOODY MARY) 1553-1558

Queen Mary I attempted to make England a Catholic nation again. Some Protestant bishops, including Archbishop Thomas Cranmer, were burnt at the stake, and other violence broke out, resulting in her being known as Bloody Mary.

QUEEN ELIZABETH I: 1558-1603

The daughter of King Henry VIII and Anne Boleyn, Queen Elizabeth I was a popular Queen. In 1588, the English navy decisively defeated the Spanish Armada. England had many notable playwrights and poets, including William Shakespeare and Ben Jonson, during her reign. She never married and had no children.

THE HOUSE OF STUART

KING JAMES I OF ENGLAND AND VI OF SCOTLAND: 1603-1625

King James I of England was the son of Mary, Queen of Scots, and Lord Darnley. His full name was James Charles Stuart. In 1605 Guy Fawkes and his Catholic co-conspirators were captured before they could blow up the Houses of Parliament; this was known as the Gunpowder Plot. In 1611, during King James I's reign, the Authorized Version of the Bible (the King James Version) was completed. Also during King James I's reign, in 1620 the Pilgrims sailed for America in their ship *The Mayflower*.

KING CHARLES I OF GREAT BRITAIN AND IRELAND: 1625-1649

King Charles I wanted to rule without Parliament. This started a Civil War that lasted from 1642-1651. He was executed on 30 January 1649. His son who would become King Charles II went into exile. For a while, the monarch ended, replaced by the Commonwealth of England (1649-1653) and then by a Protectorate (1653-1659), in which Oliver Cromwell was the Lord Protector for much of the time. Oliver Cromwell died in 1658.

KING CHARLES II: 1660-1685

In 1651, he was crowned King of Scotland. When Richard Cromwell, Oliver Cromwell's son, abdicated as Lord Protector, King Charles II was crowned and ruled Great Britain. He was affable and was known as the Merry Monarch.

APPENDIX B: NOTES

Scene 2

Then

> *rise up, Robert, and say to Richard,* Redde rationem
> villacationis tuae.
> *(Scene 2.203-205)*

***

Peters Lukacs writes in his edition of the play:

> **Robert** = an unclear reference, uncommented on by any of the editors. Perhaps this should read **Davy**, as the Friar seems to be talking to himself.

In this book, I wrote this:

> "Then rise up, Robert, and say to Richard, *Redde rationem villicationis tuae.*"

The Latin means, "Give an account of your stewardship."

Friar Hugh ap David was talking to Owen ap Rice, who still had his hands on Guenthian. "Richard" was a name that he had given to his walking-stick, and "Robert" may be a name like Tom, Dick, or Harry that he now gave to Owen ap Rice, whose real name he did not know.

"Robert" was challenging "Richard" by seizing the wench. Now "Richard" would have to show that he was a good steward by fighting and defeating "Robert."

I, however, have to wonder if the names are reversed and the passage should read: "Then rise up, Richard, and say to Robert, *Redde rationem villicationis tuae.*" Then Richard the walking-stick would rise and challenge Robert (Owen ap Rice) to give an account of his stewardship of Guenthian.

***

"Richard" is a name that the Friar has given to his walking-stick:
Later, in Peele's play we read:

> *I and Richard my man here,*
> *are here* contra omnes gentes
> *(Scene 2, 238-239)*

The Friar means that he and his walking stick can defend themselves against all the people.
And still later, we read:

> *And Richard, my man, sir*
> *(Scene 2. 257)*

The Friar means that in hiring the Friar, Llewelyn is also hiring the Friar's walking stick.

***

Just possibly, the Friar's words to his tormentors could be a reference to a meeting of Robin Hood and King Richard I the Lionheart. Robin Hood was sometimes identified as Robert, Earl of Huntington. "Robin" could be a diminutive of "Robert."
According to Wikipedia:

> In 1598, Anthony Munday wrote a pair of plays on the Robin Hood legend, *The Downfall of Robert Earl of Huntington* and *The Death of Robert Earl of Huntington* (published 1601).

Source: "Robin Hood." Wikipedia. Accessed 15 November 2020 < https://en.wikipedia.org/wiki/Robin_Hood>.
In these plays, Robin Hood is Robert Earl of Huntingdon.

Of course, Robin Hood supported Richard the Lionheart, but Richard's absence from England allowed his brother John to gain much power and rule in England, and so Robin Hood could very well say to Richard, "Give an account of your stewardship/activities."

Or if the names "Robert" and "Richard" should be reversed, it would be King Richard I asking Robin Hood to give an account of his stewardship/activities.

Scene 6

On Flora's beds and Napae's silver down
(Scene 6, line 34)

Peter Lukacs glosses "Napae" in this way, giving the *Oxford English Dictionary* as his source:

38: ***Napae*** = ***napae*** are flower nymphs;1 normally it was swans which were described as having ***silver down***.

1. *Oxford English Dictionary* (*OED*) online.

This is from the *Oxford English Dictionary* entry for "Napaea":

A nymph who inhabits woods; (occasionally also) a mountain or river nymph.

This appeared in *The Hibernian Preceptor, Comprehending A General Introduction to all kinds of Learning. In Two Volumes.* By George Wall. Dublen. Printed by J. Jones. 1812.

The nymphs were of various orders. Over the mountains the Oreades; **over the valleys the Napae**; and over the meads, the Dryades. Naiads were fresh water nymphs, as the Nereids were of the sea.

Source: Page 80.
https://tinyurl.com/y67souwp
Bold emphasis added.
Wikipedia has this:

Napaeae

From Wikipedia, the free encyclopedia

In Greek mythology, the **Napaeae** (/nəˈpiːiː/; Ancient Greek: ναπαῖαι, from νάπη, "a wooded dell") were a type of nymph that lived in wooded valleys, glens or grottoes. Statius invoked them in his *Thebaid*, when the naiad Ismenis addresses her mortal son Krenaios:

I was held a greater goddess and the Queen of Nymphae. Where alas! is that late crowd of courtiers round thy mother's halls, where are the Napaeae that prayed to serve thee?

Here Is Some Other Information About Nymphs And The Word "Napae" That I Found Interesting:
Wikipedia has this:

Auloniad

From Wikipedia, the free encyclopedia

The names of different species of nymphs varied according to their natural abodes. The **Auloniad** (/əˈloʊniæd/; Αὐλωνιάς from the classical Greek αὐλών "valley, ravine") was a nymph who could be found in mountain pastures and vales, often in the company of Pan, the god of nature.

Eurydice, for whom Orpheus traveled into dark Hades, was an Auloniad, and it was in the valley of the Thessalian river Pineios where she met her death, indirectly, at the hands of Aristaeus. Aristaeus, son of the god Apollo and the nymph Cyrene, desired to ravish Eurydice. Either disgust or fear made the nymph run away from him without looking where she was going. Eurydice trod on a poisonous serpent and died.

Wikipedia also has this:

Anthousai

From Wikipedia, the free encyclopedia

Anthousai (Ancient Greek: Ανθούσαι from ἄνθος *ánthos*, meaning "flower, blossom") are nymphs of flowers in Greek mythology. They were described as having hair that resembled hyacinth flowers. Liriope the nymph is an example of a flower nymph.

Source: https://en.wikipedia.org/wiki/Anthousai

Wikipedia also has this:

List of ancient tribes in Thrace and Dacia

From Wikipedia, the free encyclopedia

Napae, Dacianized Scythian tribe, after whom the city of Napoca is possibly named

The below information comes from <https://cord.ung.edu/topon.html>.

NAPAE

A wooded glen in the island of Lesbos, mentioned in Strabo ix. 426. In Peele's Ed. I vi. 35. Joan speaks of the Thames as "wallowing up and down On Flora's beds and Napae's silver down."

Source: https://cord.ung.edu/topon.html

See https://cord.ung.edu for *The Compendium of Renaissance Drama*: © 1989-2016 Brian Jay Corrigan.

This a translation of Strabo's *Geography* that contains the word:

It is not worth while to speak of any of the other cities. Of those mentioned by Homer, Calliarus is no longer inhabited, it is now a well-cultivated plain. Bessa, a sort of plain, does not now exist. It has its name from an accidental quality, for it abounds with woods. χώραν ἔχουσι σκαρφιεῖς, &c. It ought to be written with a double s, for it has its name from Bessa, a wooded valley, like Napē, in the plain of Methymna, which Hellanicus, through ignorance of the local circumstances, improperly calls Lapē; but the demus in Attica, from which the burghers are called Besæenses, is written with a single s. [6]

Source:
Strabo, *Geography*
H.C. Hamilton, Esq., W. Falconer, M.A., Ed.
https://tinyurl.com/y363r8y8
This is from the article titled "Nymph" in *The Ancient History Enclopedia*:

A **nymph** (**Greek**: νύμφη, *nymphē*) in Greek and in **Roman mythology** is a young female deity typically identified with natural features such as mountains (*oreads*), trees and flowers (*dryads* and *meliae*), springs, rivers and lakes (*naiads*) or the sea (*nereids*), or as part of the divine retinue of a comparable god such as **Apollo**, **Dionysos** or **Pan**, or goddesses, such as **Artemis**, who was known as the tutelary deity of all nymphs.

Source: https://www.ancient.eu/nymph/

This is from the article titled "MELIAI" at www.theoi.com:

THE MELIAI (Meliae) were the Oread-nymphs of mountain ash-tree, born of Gaia (Gaea, the Earth) when she was impregnated by the blood of the castrated Ouranos (Uranus, the Sky).

Source:

https://www.theoi.com/Nymphe/NymphaiMeliai.html

Scene 7
And Maddock toll thy passing-bell.

(Scene 7, line 33)

The line is said by Lluellen.

I have to wonder if "Maddock" is a typo for "Mannock."

Rice ap Meredith would ring the Friar's knell, and the mountain's echo would ring the Friar's passing-bell.

A passing-bell rings to announce a person's death, and a knell is a bell ringing during a funeral. In that case, the two would be much the same — the ringing and its echo — because the Friar has just "died," and his "funeral" is being held.

An argument against this, however, is that everywhere else the mountain is called "Mannock-deny," not just "Mannock."

This is Peter Lukacs' note on this line:

33: Maddock = the quartos print Maddocke; Hook wonders if this is a reference to Madog ap Llywelyn, a Welshman who would go on to lead a third rebellion against Edward in 1294-5; yay or nay, the name does not appear again in the play.

This third Welsh rebellion, led by Madog, actually resulted in an English invasion of Wales that was even larger than Edward's first two attacks of 1277 and 1282. Needless to say, Edward once again was successful in crushing the pesky Welsh rebels.

There was also a rare word maddock, which means maggot or earthworm.1,7

Scene 10

"Quo semel est imbuta recens servabit odorem
Testa diu."

(Scene 10, lines 368-369)

The Latin means, "A jar will long retain the odor of what it was dipped in when new."

Mayoress Mary was quoting Horace's *Epistles* (Book 1, Epistle 2, lines 69-70. The translation used in this book is by A.S. Kline (copyright 2005),

except I changed the British spelling "odour" to the American spelling "odor."
The use of these lines is consistent with Fair Use.

Scene 25

"*L'orecchie abbassa, come vinto e staneo*

"*Destrier c'ha in boeca il fren, gli sproni al fianco,* —

(Scene 25, lines 249-250, spoken by King Edward I)

This is William Stewart Rose's translation of the above two lines from Canto XX, stanza 131, of the Italian epic poem *Orlando Furioso*, which was written by Lodovico Ariosto:

"Stands like tired courser, who in pensive fit,

"Hangs down his ears, controlled by spur and bit"

Source: Rose, William Stewart, trans. *Orlando Furioso*. London: Henry G. Bohn, 1858.

***

"*O sommo Dio, come I giudicii umani*

"*Spesso offuscati son da un nembo oscuro!*"

(Scene 25, lines 251-252, spoken by King Edward I)

This is William Stewart Rose's translation of the above two lines from Canto X, stanza 15, of the Italian epic poem *Orlando Furioso*, which was written by Lodovico Ariosto:

"Almighty God, how fallible and vain,

"Is human judgment, dimmed by clouds obscure!"

Source: Rose, William Stewart, trans. *Orlando Furioso*. London: Henry G. Bohn, 1858.

Peter Lukacs, editor of *Edward I*, notes: "We note that the quartos print an epically mangled version of all these Italian lines."

APPENDIX C: ABOUT THE AUTHOR

It was a dark and stormy night. Suddenly a cry rang out, and on a hot summer night in 1954, Josephine, wife of Carl Bruce, gave birth to a boy — me. Unfortunately, this young married couple allowed Reuben Saturday, Josephine's brother, to name their first-born. Reuben, aka "The Joker," decided that Bruce was a nice name, so he decided to name me Bruce Bruce. I have gone by my middle name — David — ever since.

Being named Bruce David Bruce hasn't been all bad. Bank tellers remember me very quickly, so I don't often have to show an ID. It can be fun in charades, also. When I was a counselor as a teenager at Camp Echoing Hills in Warsaw, Ohio, a fellow counselor gave the signs for "sounds like" and "two words," then she pointed to a bruise on her leg twice. Bruise Bruise? Oh yeah, Bruce Bruce is the answer!

Uncle Reuben, by the way, gave me a haircut when I was in kindergarten. He cut my hair short and shaved a small bald spot on the back of my head. My mother wouldn't let me go to school until the bald spot grew out again.

Of all my brothers and sisters (six in all), I am the only transplant to Athens, Ohio. I was born in Newark, Ohio, and have lived all around Southeastern Ohio. However, I moved to Athens to go to Ohio University and have never left.

At Ohio U, I never could make up my mind whether to major in English or Philosophy, so I got a bachelor's degree with a double major in both areas, then I added a Master of Arts degree in English and a Master of Arts degree in Philosophy. Yes, I have my MAMA degree.

Currently, and for a long time to come (I eat fruits and veggies), I am spending my retirement writing books such as *Nadia Comaneci: Perfect 10*, *The Funniest People in Dance*, *Homer's* Iliad: *A Retelling in Prose*, and *William Shakespeare's* Othello: *A Retelling in Prose*.

By the way, my sister Brenda Kennedy writes romances such as *A New Beginning* and *Shattered Dreams*.

APPENDIX D: SOME BOOKS BY DAVID BRUCE

Retellings of a Classic Work of Literature

Arden of Faversham: *A Retelling*

Ben Jonson's The Alchemist: *A Retelling*

Ben Jonson's The Arraignment, or Poetaster: *A Retelling*

Ben Jonson's Bartholomew Fair: *A Retelling*

Ben Jonson's The Case is Altered: *A Retelling*

Ben Jonson's Catiline's Conspiracy: *A Retelling*

Ben Jonson's The Devil is an Ass: *A Retelling*

Ben Jonson's Epicene: *A Retelling*

Ben Jonson's Every Man in His Humor: *A Retelling*

Ben Jonson's Every Man Out of His Humor: *A Retelling*

Ben Jonson's The Fountain of Self-Love, or Cynthia's Revels: *A Retelling*

Ben Jonson's The Magnetic Lady, or Humors Reconciled: *A Retelling*

Ben Jonson's The New Inn, or The Light Heart: *A Retelling*

Ben Jonson's Sejanus' Fall: *A Retelling*

Ben Jonson's The Staple of News: *A Retelling*

Ben Jonson's A Tale of a Tub: *A Retelling*

Ben Jonson's Volpone, or the Fox: *A Retelling*

Christopher Marlowe's Complete Plays: Retellings

Christopher Marlowe's Dido, Queen of Carthage: *A Retelling*

Christopher Marlowe's Doctor Faustus: *Retellings of the 1604 A-Text and of the 1616 B-Text*

Christopher Marlowe's Edward II: *A Retelling*

Christopher Marlowe's The Massacre at Paris: *A Retelling*

Christopher Marlowe's The Rich Jew of Malta: *A Retelling*

Christopher Marlowe's Tamburlaine, Parts 1 and 2: *Retellings*

Dante's Divine Comedy: *A Retelling in Prose*

Dante's Inferno: *A Retelling in Prose*

Dante's Purgatory: *A Retelling in Prose*

Dante's Paradise: *A Retelling in Prose*

The Famous Victories of Henry V: *A Retelling*

From the Iliad *to the* Odyssey: *A Retelling in Prose of Quintus of Smyrna's* Posthomerica

George Chapman, Ben Jonson, and John Marston's Eastward Ho! *A Retelling*

George Peele's The Arraignment of Paris: *A Retelling*

George Peele's The Battle of Alcazar: *A Retelling*

George Peele's David and Bathsheba, and the Tragedy of Absalom: *A Retelling*

George Peele's Edward I: *A Retelling*

George Peele's The Old Wives' Tale: *A Retelling*

William Shakespeare's 38 Plays: Retellings in Prose
William Shakespeare's 1 Henry IV, aka Henry IV, Part 1: *A Retelling in Prose*
William Shakespeare's 2 Henry IV, aka Henry IV, Part 2: *A Retelling in Prose*
William Shakespeare's 1 Henry VI, aka Henry VI, Part 1: *A Retelling in Prose*
William Shakespeare's 2 Henry VI, aka Henry VI, Part 2: *A Retelling in Prose*
William Shakespeare's 3 Henry VI, aka Henry VI, Part 3: *A Retelling in Prose*
William Shakespeare's All's Well that Ends Well: *A Retelling in Prose*
William Shakespeare's Antony and Cleopatra: *A Retelling in Prose*
William Shakespeare's As You Like It: *A Retelling in Prose*
William Shakespeare's The Comedy of Errors: *A Retelling in Prose*
William Shakespeare's Coriolanus: *A Retelling in Prose*
William Shakespeare's Cymbeline: *A Retelling in Prose*
William Shakespeare's Hamlet: *A Retelling in Prose*
William Shakespeare's Henry V: *A Retelling in Prose*
William Shakespeare's Henry VIII: *A Retelling in Prose*
William Shakespeare's Julius Caesar: *A Retelling in Prose*
William Shakespeare's King John: *A Retelling in Prose*
William Shakespeare's King Lear: *A Retelling in Prose*
William Shakespeare's Love's Labor's Lost: *A Retelling in Prose*
William Shakespeare's Macbeth: *A Retelling in Prose*
William Shakespeare's Measure for Measure: *A Retelling in Prose*
William Shakespeare's The Merchant of Venice: *A Retelling in Prose*
William Shakespeare's The Merry Wives of Windsor: *A Retelling in Prose*
William Shakespeare's A Midsummer Night's Dream: *A Retelling in Prose*
William Shakespeare's Much Ado About Nothing: *A Retelling in Prose*
William Shakespeare's Othello: *A Retelling in Prose*
William Shakespeare's Pericles, Prince of Tyre: *A Retelling in Prose*
William Shakespeare's Richard II: *A Retelling in Prose*
William Shakespeare's Richard III: *A Retelling in Prose*
William Shakespeare's Romeo and Juliet: *A Retelling in Prose*
William Shakespeare's The Taming of the Shrew: *A Retelling in Prose*
William Shakespeare's The Tempest: *A Retelling in Prose*
William Shakespeare's Timon of Athens: *A Retelling in Prose*
William Shakespeare's Titus Andronicus: *A Retelling in Prose*
William Shakespeare's Troilus and Cressida: *A Retelling in Prose*
William Shakespeare's Twelfth Night: *A Retelling in Prose*
William Shakespeare's The Two Gentlemen of Verona: *A Retelling in Prose*
William Shakespeare's The Two Noble Kinsmen: *A Retelling in Prose*
William Shakespeare's The Winter's Tale: *A Retelling in Prose*